William Shakespeare'
The Merchant of Venice
In Plain and Simple English

BookCaps Study Guides
www.bookcaps.com

© 2011. All Rights Reserved.

Table of Contents

About This Series 3

Characters 4

Play 5

   Act I 6

      SCENE I. Venice. A street. 7

      SCENE II: Belmont. A room in PORTIA'S house. 15

      SCENE III. Venice. A public place. 21

   Act II 29

      SCENE I. Belmont. A room in PORTIA'S house. 30

      SCENE II. Venice. A street. 32

      SCENE III. The same. A room in SHYLOCK'S house. 41

      SCENE IV. The same. A street. 42

      SCENE V. The same. Before SHYLOCK'S house. 45

      SCENE VI. The same. 48

      SCENE VII. Belmont. A room in PORTIA'S house. 52

      SCENE VIII. Venice. A street. 55

   Act III 61

      SCENE I. Venice. A street. 62

      SCENE II. Belmont. A room in PORTIA'S house. 68

      SCENE III. Venice. A street. 80

      SCENE IV. Belmont. A room in PORTIA'S house 82

      SCENE V. The same. A garden 85

   Act IV 89

      SCENE I. Venice. A court of justice. 90

      SCENE II. The same. A street. 109

   Act V 111

      SCENE I. Belmont. Avenue to PORTIA'S house. 112

About This Series

The "Classic Retold" series started as a way of telling classics for the modern reader—being careful to preserve the themes and integrity of the original. Whether you want to understand Shakespeare a little more or are trying to get a better grasps of the Greek classics, there is a book waiting for you!

The series is expanding every month. Visit BookCaps.com to see all the books in the series, and while you are there join the Facebook page, so you are first to know when a new book comes out.

Characters

THE DUKE OF VENICE

THE PRINCE OF MOROCCO, suitor to Portia

THE PRINCE OF ARRAGON, suitor to Portia

ANTONIO, a merchant of Venice

BASSANIO, his friend

SALANIO, friend to Antonio and Bassanio

GRATIANO, friend to Antonio and Bassanio

LORENZO, in love with Jessica

SHYLOCK, a rich Jew

TUBAL, a Jew, his friend

LAUNCELOT GOBBO, a clown, servant to Shylock

OLD GOBBO, father to Launcelot

LEONARDO, servant to Bassanio

BALTHASAR, servant to Portia

STEPHANO, servant to Portia

PORTIA, a rich heiress

NERISSA, her waiting-maid

JESSICA, daughter to Shylock

Magnificoes of Venice, Officers of the Court of Justice,

Gaoler, Servants to Portia, and other Attendants

Play

Act I

SCENE I. Venice. A street.

Enter ANTONIO, SALARINO, and SALANIO

ANTONIO
In sooth, I know not why I am so sad:
It wearies me; you say it wearies you;
But how I caught it, found it, or came by it,
What stuff 'tis made of, whereof it is born, —
I am to learn;
And such a want-wit sadness makes of me,
That I have much ado to know myself.

SALARINO
Your mind is tossing on the ocean;
There, where your argosies with portly sail,
Like signiors and rich burghers on the flood,
Or, as it were, the pageants of the sea,
Do overpeer the petty traffickers,

That curtsy to them, do them reverence,
As they fly by them with their woven wings.

SALANIO
Believe me, sir, had I such venture forth,

The better part of my affections would
Be with my hopes abroad. I should be still
Plucking the grass, to know where sits the wind,

Peering in maps for ports and piers and roads;

And every object that might make me fear
Misfortune to my ventures, out of doubt

Would make me sad.

SALARINO
My wind cooling my broth
Would blow me to an ague, when I thought
What harm a wind too great at sea might do.

I should not see the sandy hour-glass run,

	I have no idea why I am so sad. It tires me and you say it tires you, too. And how I came about being so sad-- Whatever it's about and where it comes from I do not know. It all makes me feel so stupid, And I have to make it my business to know myself.
	You're thinking about the ocean, And wondering how your ships are doing. They are fine, like citizens on the deep waves, Or like a play out on the sea— They are large and look down on the smaller ships That bow to them and pay them respects As they fly past with their elegant sails.
	Trust me, if I had dealings going on like you do Most all of my thoughts and attention would Be on the business overseas. I would be Plucking up blades of grass to figure out which way the wind blows, And peering at maps looking for ports and piers and roads. Any little thing that might make me afraid Of bad luck taking over my business would fill me with doubt And that would make me so sad.
	Blowing on my soup to cool it Would make me feel so upset because I'd think Of the harm a strong wind at sea might do to my ships. I wouldn't be able to look at sand in an hourglass,

But I should think of shallows and of flats,	Without worrying about shallow waters with sandbars.
And see my wealthy Andrew dock'd in sand,	I'd see my majestic ship Andrew docked in the sand,
Vailing her high-top lower than her ribs To kiss her burial. Should I go to church And see the holy edifice of stone, And not bethink me straight of dangerous rocks,	Upside down with the sails in the water Sinking to her death. If I were to go to church I'd see the stones it is made of, And I couldn't help but think of dangerous rocks
Which touching but my gentle vessel's side, Would scatter all her spices on the stream,	Which could split the sides of my ship Scattering all the spices in the hold into the ocean,
Enrobe the roaring waters with my silks, And, in a word, but even now worth this, And now worth nothing? Shall I have the thought To think on this, and shall I lack the thought That such a thing bechanced would make me sad?	And tossing the silks inside upon the waves. In an instant I'd be worth nothing. How could I have these thoughts about all that could go wrong and not worry? The things I'd imagine that could happen would make me so sad.
But tell not me; I know, Antonio Is sad to think upon his merchandise.	You don't have to tell me—I know, Antonio Is sad to think of all that could happen to his merchandise.
ANTONIO Believe me, no: I thank my fortune for it,	No, trust me, that's not it. I am financially stable
My ventures are not in one bottom trusted,	And I don't have everything invested in one ship,
Nor to one place; nor is my whole estate	Or in one place. My finances are not dependent
Upon the fortune of this present year: Therefore my merchandise makes me not sad.	On how well I do this year. So, it's not the merchandise in the ships making me sad.
SALARINO Why, then you are in love.	Well, then, you must be in love.
ANTONIO Fie, fie!	Get out of here!
SALARINO Not in love neither? Then let us say you are sad,	Not in love, either? Well let's just say you are sad
Because you are not merry: and 'twere as easy	Because you are not happy. It would be just as easy
For you to laugh and leap and say you are merry,	For you to laugh and dance and say you are happy

Because you are not sad. Now, by two-headed Janus, Nature hath framed strange fellows in her time: Some that will evermore peep through their eyes And laugh like parrots at a bag-piper, And other of such vinegar aspect That they'll not show their teeth in way of smile, Though Nestor swear the jest be laughable.	*Because you are not sad.* *Humans have two faces* *and many people have strange ways of* *expressing moods.* *Some will look out at the world* *and laugh at just about anything,* *While others are so sour and bitter* *They won't ever crack a smile* *Even at the funniest jokes in the world.*

Enter BASSANIO, LORENZO, and GRATIANO

SALANIO Here comes Bassanio, your most noble kinsman, Gratiano and Lorenzo. Fare ye well: We leave you now with better company.	*Here comes your cousin Bassanio,* *and Gratiano and Lorenzo. We'll see you* *later-* *They'll be better company for you.*
SALARINO I would have stay'd till I had made you merry, If worthier friends had not prevented me.	*I would have stayed until I cheered you up,* *If friends you are closer to hadn't shown up.*
ANTONIO Your worth is very dear in my regard. I take it, your own business calls on you And you embrace the occasion to depart.	*You are worth much to me in that way.* *I'm thinking your own business needs you* *And you are taking the chance to leave.*
SALARINO Good morrow, my good lords.	*Hello, my good men!*
BASSANIO Good signiors both, when shall we laugh? say, when? You grow exceeding strange: must it be so?	*Hello, both of you. When will we get together* *for fun? When?* *I never see you these days. Does it have to be* *that way?*
SALARINO We'll make our leisures to attend on yours.	*We'll be available whenever you want to get* *together.*

Exeunt Salarino and Salanio

LORENZO My Lord Bassanio, since you have found Antonio, We two will leave you: but at dinner-time, I pray you, have in mind where we must meet.	*Bassanio, since you have found Antonio,* *We will go ahead. But at dinner time* *Don't forget we're getting together.*

BASSANIO
I will not fail you.

No problem, I'll be there.

GRATIANO
You look not well, Signior Antonio;
You have too much respect upon the world:
They lose it that do buy it with much care:
Believe me, you are marvellously changed.

You don't look so good, Antonio.
You take the world too seriously.
You don't gain anything by investing so much.
Trust me, you don't seem quite yourself.

ANTONIO
I hold the world but as the world, Gratiano;
A stage where every man must play a part,
And mine a sad one.

The world is just the world, Gratiano.
A stage where every man must play a part,
And mine is a sad one.

GRATIANO
Let me play the fool:
With mirth and laughter let old wrinkles come,
And let my liver rather heat with wine
Than my heart cool with mortifying groans.
Why should a man, whose blood is warm within,
Sit like his grandsire cut in alabaster?

Sleep when he wakes and creep into the jaundice

By being peevish? I tell thee what, Antonio--

I love thee, and it is my love that speaks--

There are a sort of men whose visages
Do cream and mantle like a standing pond,

And do a wilful stillness entertain,
With purpose to be dress'd in an opinion
Of wisdom, gravity, profound conceit,
As who should say 'I am Sir Oracle,
And when I ope my lips let no dog bark!'

O my Antonio, I do know of these
That therefore only are reputed wise
For saying nothing; when, I am very sure,
If they should speak,
would almost damn those ears,
Which, hearing them, would call their

Well then let me play the fool's part:
I will have fun and laugh until I am wrinkled.
And let me ruin my liver with wine
Rather than my heart be ruined with crying.
Why should a man whose blood is warm
Sit still like the statue of his grandfather
carved in stone?
Why should he sleep when he is awake and
grow sickly
From being irritable? I'll tell you what,
Antonio-
I love you, and it is my love that speaks when I
say
There is a type of man whose face
Becomes frothy and scummy like a stagnant
pond,
Who is purposely silent and still,
To try to make others see them as
Wise, respected and important,
As if they are saying 'I am Mr. Wiseman,
And when I open my mouth, dogs should stop
barking!'
Antonio, I know of many men
Who are thought to be very wise
Simply by saying nothing, but I'm sure
If they were to speak,
it would be painful to hear
And those hearing them would see them as

brothers fools. I'll tell thee more of this another time: But fish not, with this melancholy bait, For this fool gudgeon, this opinion. Come, good Lorenzo. Fare ye well awhile: I'll end my exhortation after dinner.	*fools.* *I'll talk more about this some other time.* *But for now, stop looking for sadness* *It's foolish to do so, in my opinion.* *Come on, Lorenzo, let's go.* *I'll say more about this after dinner.*

LORENZO
Well, we will leave you then till dinner-time: I must be one of these same dumb wise men, For Gratiano never lets me speak.	*Well, we will see you at dinner time:* *I must be one of these dumb wise men* *Because Gratiano never lets me speak.*

GRATIANO
Well, keep me company but two years moe, Thou shalt not know the sound of thine own tongue.	*Well, hang out with me for another couple of years* *And you won't even recognize the sound of your own voice.*

ANTONIO
Farewell: I'll grow a talker for this gear.	*See you later. I'll become a talker after all of this!*

GRATIANO
Thanks, i' faith, for silence is only commendable In a neat's tongue dried and a maid not vendible.	*Thanks, and trust me, silence is only good* *In a cow's tongue that's ready to eat or that of an old maid.*

Exeunt GRATIANO and LORENZO

ANTONIO
Is that any thing now?	*Is that important what he says?*

BASSANIO
Gratiano speaks an infinite deal of nothing, more than any man in all Venice. His reasons are as two grains of wheat hid in two bushels of chaff: you shall seek all day ere you find them, and when you have them, they are not worth the search.	*Gratiano says a lot about nothing, more* *Than any other man in Venice. The point he tries to make* *Is like two grains of wheat hidden in a haystack: you* *Spend the whole day looking for them and once* *You find them, you realize they weren't worth the trouble.*

ANTONIO
Well, tell me now what lady is the same To whom you swore a secret pilgrimage, That you to-day promised to tell me of?	*So, tell me now who is the girl* *You're taking a secret trip to see?* *The one you promised to tell me about today?*

BASSANIO
'Tis not unknown to you, Antonio,
How much I have disabled mine estate,
By something showing a more swelling port
Than my faint means would grant continuance:
Nor do I now make moan to be abridged
From such a noble rate; but my chief care

Is to come fairly off from the great debts
Wherein my time something too prodigal
Hath left me gaged. To you, Antonio,
I owe the most, in money and in love,

And from your love I have a warranty

To unburden all my plots and purposes
How to get clear of all the debts I owe.

ANTONIO
I pray you, good Bassanio, let me know it;
And if it stand, as you yourself still do,
Within the eye of honour, be assured,
My purse, my person, my extremest means,
Lie all unlock'd to your occasions.

BASSANIO
In my school-days, when I had lost one shaft,
I shot his fellow of the self-same flight

The self-same way with more advised watch,
To find the other forth, and by adventuring both

I oft found both: I urge this childhood proof,

Because what follows is pure innocence.

I owe you much, and, like a wilful youth,
That which I owe is lost; but if you please

To shoot another arrow that self way
Which you did shoot the first, I do not doubt,

As I will watch the aim, or to find both

Well, as you know, Antonio
I've more or less ruined my finances
By living the high life
and spending way beyond my means.
I'm not complaining about have to cut back
From what I was used to spending, and my main concern
Is to be able to pay off all of the debts
that all that time of extravagant overspending
left me with. To you, Antonio,
I owe the most, in both money and appreciation,
And because of your kindness I feel it is my duty
To share with you my plan
For clearing myself of the debts I owe.

Please, Bassanio, tell me your plan
And if it sounds solid, as you yourself do,
On my word, you can be certain
That my money, myself and anything I can do
for you are at your disposal to help you.

Back when I was in school, if I lost an arrow
I would shoot another one in the same direction
In the exact same way, but I'd watch it closer
In order to find the first one, and by shooting both
I found both, most of the time. I tell you this story
Because what I'm about to say may sound silly.
I owe you a lot, and like a stubborn child,
I lost everything I owe you. But if you are willing
To shoot another arrow in the same direction
As the first one you shot for me, I have no doubt
I will watch where it goes and find both

Or bring your latter hazard back again	Or, at the very least, bring the second one back
And thankfully rest debtor for the first.	And only owe you for the first.

ANTONIO
You know me well, and herein spend but time	You know me well, and you are spending too much time
To wind about my love with circumstance;	Going on about our friendship with such detail.
And out of doubt you do me now more wrong	You're doing more harm by doubting our friendship
In making question of my uttermost	And making me wonder about us now
Than if you had made waste of all I have:	Than if you had destroyed all that I have.
Then do but say to me what I should do	Just tell me what it is you need me to do
That in your knowledge may by me be done,	And as long as you know I am capable of doing it,
And I am prest unto it: therefore, speak.	I will do it. So, just tell me what you need.

BASSANIO
In Belmont is a lady richly left;	In Belmont there is a woman who has inherited a lot of money
And she is fair, and, fairer than that word,	And she is beautiful, and even better than that,
Of wondrous virtues: sometimes from her eyes	She is a good person. Sometimes the way she looks at me
I did receive fair speechless messages:	Makes me think she is trying to let me know she likes me.
Her name is Portia, nothing undervalued	Her name is Portia, and she is no less valuable
To Cato's daughter, Brutus' Portia:	Than the Portia who is Cato's daughter and married to Brutus:
Nor is the wide world ignorant of her worth,	The whole world knows how wealthy she is,
For the four winds blow in from every coast	And the four winds from every direction blow in, Famous suitors, and her blond hair
Renowned suitors, and her sunny locks	
Hang on her temples like a golden fleece;	Falls in her face like the golden fleece in the Greek myth,
Which makes her seat of Belmont Colchos' strand,	And her estate on the coast of Belmont is like Colchos,
And many Jasons come in quest of her.	And many men come to win her, like Jason in the myth.
O my Antonio, had I but the means	Antonio, if I only had the money
To hold a rival place with one of them,	To hold my own against them,
I have a mind presages me such thrift,	I know in my mind I could win her heart,
That I should questionless be fortunate!	And I have no doubt I'd be successful!

ANTONIO
Thou know'st that all my fortunes are at sea;

Neither have I money nor commodity

To raise a present sum: therefore go forth;
Try what my credit can in Venice do:

That shall be rack'd, even to the uttermost,
To furnish thee to Belmont, to fair Portia.

Go, presently inquire, and so will I,
Where money is, and I no question make

To have it of my trust or for my sake.

Exeunt

You know that all my money is invested in my ships,
And I don't have the money on hand or the goods
To raise the cash you need. So, let's go
And see what my good credit in Venice can drum up:
We'll get as big a loan as possible
To provide what you need to get to Belmont and beautiful Portia.
Go ask around, and so will I,
Let's find out where the money is and I won't hesitate
To sign for it in my name.

SCENE II: Belmont. A room in PORTIA'S house.

Enter PORTIA and NERISSA

PORTIA
By my troth, Nerissa, my little body is aweary of this great world.

My word, but my little body is so tired of this big world.

NERISSA
You would be, sweet madam, if your miseries were in the same abundance as your good fortunes are: and yet, for aught I see, they are as sick that surfeit with too much as they that starve with nothing. It is no mean happiness therefore, to be seated in the mean: superfluity comes sooner by white hairs, but competency lives longer.

You would be tired, as well, if your troubles were in the same proportion as your fortunes are, and yet, from what I see, people who have too much get as sick from having too much as those who starve and have nothing. It is no small happiness, therefore, to be right in the middle: having too much ages one faster, while having just enough extends your life.

PORTIA
Good sentences and well pronounced.

True words, and well spoken.

NERISSA
They would be better, if well followed.

They would be even better if you followed them.

PORTIA
If to do were as easy as to know what were good to do, chapels had been churches and poor men's cottages princes' palaces. It is a good divine that follows his own instructions: I can easier teach twenty what were good to be done, than be one of the twenty to follow mine own teaching. The brain may devise laws for the blood, but a hot temper leaps o'er a cold decree: such a hare is madness the

If it were as easy to do as it is to know what good to do, small chapels would be great churches and poor men's cottages would become prince's palaces. It is a good priest who follows his own instructions: I can easier teach twenty people of the good that can be done than be one of the twenty to follow my own teaching. The brain can come up with laws for the blood, but a hot temper overtakes a well-thought out decision: just like a rabbit,

youth, to skip o'er the meshes of good counsel the

cripple. But this reasoning is not in the fashion to

choose me a husband.
O me, the word 'choose!' I may
neither choose whom I would nor refuse whom I
dislike; so is the will of a living daughter curbed

by the will of a dead father. Is it not hard,
Nerissa, that I cannot choose one nor refuse none?

NERISSA
Your father was ever virtuous;
and holy men at their
death have good inspirations: therefore the lottery,

that he hath devised in these three chests of gold,

silver and lead, whereof who chooses his meaning

chooses you, will, no doubt,
never be chosen by any
rightly but one who shall rightly love. But what
warmth is there in your affection towards any of
these princely suitors that are already come?

PORTIA
I pray thee, over-name them; and as thou namest

them, I will describe them; and, according to my
description, level at my affection.

NERISSA
First, there is the Neapolitan prince.

PORTIA
Ay, that's a colt indeed, for he doth nothing but

talk of his horse; and he makes it a great
appropriation to his own good parts, that he can
shoe him himself. I am much afeard my lady his
mother played false with a smith.

---

young people jump over the nets of good advice
held by crippled old men. But thinking in this way is not the sort that
will help choose a husband.
Oh, my! The word 'choose!' I cannot choose who I'd like or refuse who I don't like; such is the fate of a living daughter restricted
by the wishes of a dead father. It's hard, isn't it, Nerissa, that I can't choose one or refuse any?

Your father was a good man,
and religious men at their
death sometimes have well-intentioned ideas, and that's why we have the lottery
he came up with using these three trunks of gold,
silver and lead, where whoever can figure out the right answer
chooses you and the trunk won't, don't doubt it, be chosen by any
except the one who is right for you. But are you having warm feelings toward any of these princely suitors that have already arrived?

I'll tell you what—go over their names, and as you name
them, I will describe them, and according to my description you will be able to guess how I feel about them.

First, there is the Neapolitan prince.

Yes, now there's a foolish youth, for sure, who does nothing but
talk about his horse, and he makes a big deal that he has the unique ability of being able to shoe the horse himself. I very much fear the Woman who is his mother had an affair with a blacksmith.

NERISSA
Then there is the County Palatine.

Next is the County Palatine.

PORTIA
He doth nothing but frown,
as who should say 'If you
will not have me, choose:' he hears merry tales and
smiles not: I fear he will prove the weeping
philosopher when he grows old, being so full of
unmannerly sadness in his youth. I had rather be
married to a death's-head with a bone in his mouth
than to either of these. God defend me from these
two!

He does nothing but frown, as if to say 'If you do not choose me, I do not care.' He hears happy stories and does not smile at them: I suspect he will be the sad philosopher when he grows old since he is so full of inappropriate sadness in his youth. I would rather be married to a skull with a bone in it mouth than to either of these. God forbid I end up with one of them!

NERISSA
How say you by the French lord,
Monsieur Le Bon?

What do you think about the French lord, Monsieur Le Bon?

PORTIA
God made him,
and therefore let him pass for a man.
In truth, I know it is a sin to be a mocker: but,
he! why, he hath a horse better than the
Neapolitan's, a better bad habit of frowning than
the Count Palatine; he is every man in no man; if a
throstle sing, he falls straight a capering: he will
fence with his own shadow:
if I should marry him, I
should marry twenty husbands.
If he would despise me
I would forgive him, for if he love me to madness,
I shall never requite him.

God made him so let's call him a man. Truth be told, I know it is a sin to make fun of people, but him! He has a horse better than the prince for Naples and a better way of frowning than the Count Palatine; he is every man you'd want in no man. If a bird begins to sing, he begins to prance; he will fence with his own shadow If I were to marry him I would marry twenty husbands. It he were to hate me I would forgive him, and if he were to love me to madness, I would never give him the same love.

NERISSA
What say you, then, to Falconbridge,
the young baron of England?

Well, what do you say about Falconbridge, the young baron of England?

PORTIA
You know I say nothing to him, for he understands not me, nor I him: he hath neither Latin, French, nor Italian, and you will come into the court and swear that I have a poor pennyworth in the English. He is a proper man's picture, but, alas, who can converse with a dumb-show?
How oddly he is suited!
I think he bought his doublet in Italy, his round hose in France, his bonnet in Germany and his behavior every where.

	I really have nothing to say about him because he does not understand me, and I don't understand him. He doesn't speak Latin, French, or Italian, and anyone in the court knows I don't know English of any value at all. He's really good looking, but who can talk with someone who doesn't understand them? And he was dressed so weirdly! He must have bought his jacket in Italy, his tights in France, his hat in Germany and his way of behaving everywhere.

NERISSA
What think you of the Scottish lord, his neighbour?

What do you think of his neighbor, the Scottish lord?

PORTIA
That he hath a neighbourly charity in him, for he borrowed a box of the ear of the Englishman and swore he would pay him again when he was able: I think the Frenchman became his surety and sealed under for another.

I think he has a neighborly generosity about him, because he took a slap to the ear by the Englishman and swore he would pay him back as soon as he was able. I think the Frenchman guaranteed he would help the Scotsman and then added a slap of his own.

NERISSA
How like you the young German, the Duke of Saxony's nephew?

How do you like the young German, the Duke of Saxony's nephew?

PORTIA
Very vilely in the morning, when he is sober, and most vilely in the afternoon, when he is drunk: when he is best, he is a little worse than a man, and when he is worst, he is little better than a beast: and the worst fall that ever fell, I hope I shall make shift to go without him.

He's pretty wretched in the morning, when he is sober, and even more so in the afternoon, when he is drunk: when he is best, he is a little worse than a man, and when he is worst, he is not much better than an animal: if he where to die, I would think I could do okay without him.

Original	Modern
NERISSA If he should offer to choose, and choose the right casket, you should refuse to perform your father's will, if you should refuse to accept him.	If he wants to try and choose and he chooses the right box, you would be refusing to go by what your father wants if you were to refuse to marry him.
PORTIA Therefore, for fear of the worst, I pray thee, set a deep glass of rhenish wine on the contrary casket, for if the devil be within and that temptation without, I know he will choose it. I will do any thing, Nerissa, ere I'll be married to a sponge.	I know, so for fear of the worst, let me ask you to place a huge glass of German white wine on the wrong box so that even if it is the wrong one he will be tempted by the wine and I know he would choose it. I will do anything, Nerissa, before I marry a drunk.
NERISSA You need not fear, lady, the having any of these lords: they have acquainted me with their determinations; which is, indeed, to return to their home and to trouble you with no more suit, unless you may be won by some other sort than your father's imposition depending on the caskets.	You don't have to worry about having any of these suitors: they have all told me their decision is to, indeed, return to their home and to not try to win you unless you may be won in some other way than your father's command that they choose the correct box.
PORTIA If I live to be as old as Sibylla, I will die as chaste as Diana, unless I be obtained by the manner of my father's will. I am glad this parcel of wooers are so reasonable, for there is not one among them but I dote on his very absence, and I pray God grant them a fair departure.	If I live to be as old as Sibylla, I will die an old maid unless I am won in the manner my father has willed. I am glad this group of wooers is so reasonable as to leave because there is not one of them I care about except for their absence, so I wish them all a good departure.
NERISSA Do you not remember, lady, in your father's time, a Venetian, a scholar and a soldier, that came hither in company of the Marquis of Montferrat?	Do you remember when your father was alive, a Venetian—a scholar and a soldier—who came her in the company of the Marquis of Montferrat?
PORTIA Yes, yes, it was Bassanio; as I think, he was so called.	Yes, yes I do. That was Bassanio, at least I think that was his name.

NERISSA
True, madam: he,
of all the men that ever my foolish
eyes looked upon, was the best deserving
a fair lady.

PORTIA
I remember him well, and I remember him
worthy of thy praise.
Enter a Serving-man

How now! what news?

Servant
The four strangers seek for you, madam, to take

their leave: and there is a forerunner come from a

fifth, the Prince of Morocco, who brings word the
prince his master will be here to-night.

PORTIA
If I could bid the fifth welcome with so good a
heart as I can bid the other four farewell, I should

be glad of his approach: if he have the condition
of a saint and the complexion of a devil, I had
rather he should shrive me than wive me. Come,

Nerissa. Sirrah, go before.
Whiles we shut the gates
upon one wooer, another knocks at the door.

Exeunt

*Yes, madam: he,
of all the men that I've ever laid
eyes on, was the best and deserving of a
beautiful woman.*

*I remember him well, and I recall him being
worthy of your praise.*

What is it? What is the news?

*There are four strangers here for you, madam,
they want
to say goodbye: and there is a messenger
coming from a
fifth, the Prince of Morocco, who brings news
that the prince, his master, will be here
tonight.*

*If I could say hello to the fifth with as much
enthusiasm as I say goodbye to the other four,
I would
be glad of his arrival: if he is like
a saint but looks like a devil, I would
rather he would forgive me rather than marry
me. Come on,
Nerissa. Sir, go ahead.
While we shut the gates
upon one wooer, another one knocks at the
door.*

SCENE III. Venice. A public place.

Enter BASSANIO and SHYLOCK

SHYLOCK
Three thousand ducats; well.

Three thousand ducats, well.

BASSANIO
Ay, sir, for three months.

Yes, sir, for three months.

SHYLOCK
For three months; well.

For three months, well, let's see.

BASSANIO
For the which, as I told you,
Antonio shall be bound.

The amount of which, as I told you, Antonio will guarantee to pay.

SHYLOCK
Antonio shall become bound; well.

Antonio will guarantee it, well, let's see.

BASSANIO
May you stead me? will you pleasure me? shall I know your answer?

Will you help me? Will you gratify me? Can I know your answer?

SHYLOCK
Three thousand ducats for three months and Antonio bound.

Three thousand ducats for three months and Antonio will guarantee it.

BASSANIO
Your answer to that.

What is your answer?

SHYLOCK
Antonio is a good man.

Antonio is a good man.

BASSANIO
Have you heard any imputation to the contrary?

Have you heard anyone say anything to contradict that?

SHYLOCK
Oh, no, no, no, no: my meaning in saying he is a good man is to have you understand me that he is sufficient. Yet his means are in supposition: he

hath an argosy bound to Tripolis, another to the

Oh. No, no, no, no. What I meant when I said he is a good man is that I am saying he is sufficient. Even though his investments are tied up: he

has a ship on its way to Tripolis and another headed toward

Indies; I understand moreover, upon the Rialto, he

hath a third at Mexico, a fourth for England, and

other ventures he hath, squandered abroad. But ships
are but boards, sailors but men: there be land-rats

and water-rats, water-thieves and land-thieves, I
mean pirates, and then there is the peril of waters,

winds and rocks. The man is, notwithstanding,
sufficient. Three thousand ducats; I think I may
take his bond.

BASSANIO
Be assured you may.

SHYLOCK
I will be assured I may; and, that I may be assured,

I will bethink me. May I speak with Antonio?

BASSANIO
If it please you to dine with us.

SHYLOCK
Yes, to smell pork; to eat of the habitation which

your prophet the Nazarite conjured the devil into. I
will buy with you, sell with you, talk with you,
walk with you, and so following, but I will not eat
with you, drink with you, nor pray with you. What
news on the Rialto? Who is he comes here?

Enter ANTONIO

BASSANIO
This is Signior Antonio.

SHYLOCK
[Aside]
How like a fawning publican he looks!
I hate him for he is a Christian,

---

the Indies. I also understand, from people at Rialto, he
has a third ship at Mexico, a fourth bound for England, and
many other business ventures abroad on the seas. But ships
are just made of wood, and sailors are men. There are land rats
and water rats, water thieves and land thieves. I mean pirates, and then there is the danger of the waters,
winds and rocks. The man, despite all of this, has money. Three thousand ducats, I think I will let him guarantee it.

You can be certain you can.

I will be certain I can, and so that I might be certain,
I'll think of a way. May I speak with Antonio?

You are welcome to join us for dinner.

What, and smell pork? To eat of the sort of animal which
your prophet Jesus charmed the devil into? I will buy with you, sell with you, talk with you, walk with you, and so on, but I will not eat with you, drink with you, or pray with you. What's the news from the Rialto? Who is here now?

This is Signior Antonio.

[Aside]
He looks just like a gloating tax collector!
I hate him because he is a Christian.

But more for that in low simplicity He lends out money gratis and brings down The rate of usance here with us in Venice. If I can catch him once upon the hip, I will feed fat the ancient grudge I bear him. He hates our sacred nation, and he rails, Even there where merchants most do congregate, On me, my bargains and my well-won thrift, Which he calls interest. Cursed be my tribe, If I forgive him!	But more so because he foolishly Lends out money with no interest and brings down The rate of interest for us here in Venice. If I can just get him into an unfavorable position just once, I will satisfy the old grudge I have against him. He hates our sacred nation and he rants In the places where the merchants gather About me, and my deals and my well-earned profit That he refers to as interest. Jews everywhere would be cursed If I were to forgive him!
BASSANIO Shylock, do you hear?	Shylock, did you hear me?
SHYLOCK I am debating of my present store, And, by the near guess of my memory, I cannot instantly raise up the gross Of full three thousand ducats. What of that? Tubal, a wealthy Hebrew of my tribe, Will furnish me. But soft! how many months Do you desire?	I am thinking about how much I have on hand, And, if my memory serves me right, I can't instantly come up with the total Of the full three thousand ducats. But so what? Tubal, a wealthy jew I know will give it to me. But wait! How many months did you say you need it?
To ANTONIO Rest you fair, good signior; Your worship was the last man in our mouths.	How are you, signior? We were just talking about you.
ANTONIO Shylock, although I neither lend nor borrow By taking nor by giving of excess, Yet, to supply the ripe wants of my friend, I'll break a custom. Is he yet possess'd How much ye would?	Shylock, although I generally never lend or borrow by charging or paying interest, In order to help supply my friend's needs I will do it this time. Does he know yet how much it is you need?
SHYLOCK Ay, ay, three thousand ducats.	Oh, yes, three thousand ducats.
ANTONIO And for three months.	For three months.

SHYLOCK
I had forgot; three months; you told me so.

Well then, your bond; and let me see; but hear you;

Methought you said you neither lend nor borrow
Upon advantage.

ANTONIO
I do never use it.

SHYLOCK
When Jacob grazed his uncle Laban's sheep--

This Jacob from our holy Abram was,
As his wise mother wrought in his behalf,
The third possessor; ay, he was the third—

ANTONIO
And what of him? did he take interest?

SHYLOCK
No, not take interest, not, as you would say,

Directly interest: mark what Jacob did.

When Laban and himself were compromised
That all the eanlings which were streak'd and pied

Should fall as Jacob's hire, the ewes, being rank,

In the end of autumn turned to the rams,

And, when the work of generation was
Between these woolly breeders in the act,
The skilful shepherd peel'd me certain wands,

And, in the doing of the deed of kind,
He stuck them up before the fulsome ewes,

Who then conceiving did in eaning time
Fall parti-colour'd lambs, and those were Jacob's.

I had forgotten—three months. You told me that.

Well, then, your loan. Well, let me see. But, listen,

I thought you said you never lend or borrow with interest?

I don't.

When Jacob looked after his uncle Laban's sheep—

*Jacob, by the way, was Abram's grandson,
And his mother had set it up to his advantage
That he would be heir to Abram, yes, third in line—*

What's your point about him? Did he take interest?

No, he did not take interest, not, as you would say,

Direct interest, anyway. Listen, here is what he did:

*At the time Laban and Jacob agreed
That all the baby lambs that were multi-colored*

Would be Jacob's pay. The females were ready to breed

Since it was the end of autumn, and turning to the males.

*While the sheep were in the act of breeding,
Jacob cut and peeled multi-colored pieces of wood*

*And while the sheep were mating
He stuck the wood pieces in the ground in front of the females*

*So that they would see them while conceiving
And then bear multi-colored babies, which went to Jacob.*

This was a way to thrive, and he was blest:	This was a way to be successful and he was blessed.
And thrift is blessing, if men steal it not.	Profit is a blessing as long as you don't steal it.

ANTONIO
This was a venture, sir, that Jacob served for;	That was a business deal that Jacob worked for.
A thing not in his power to bring to pass,	It was not in his power to make it happen,
But sway'd and fashion'd by the hand of heaven.	It was influenced by the God's will.
Was this inserted to make interest good?	Are you telling this story to justify charging interest?
Or is your gold and silver ewes and rams?	Are you comparing your gold and silver to breeding sheep?

SHYLOCK
I cannot tell; I make it breed as fast:	I can't tell the difference. It multiplies just as fast. But listen to me, signior—
But note me, signior.	

ANTONIO
Mark you this, Bassanio,	Pay attention to this, Bassanio,
The devil can cite Scripture for his purpose.	The devil can cite Scripture to suit his purpose.
An evil soul producing holy witness	An evil person who brings out holy evidence
Is like a villain with a smiling cheek,	Is like a villain who smiles at you,
A goodly apple rotten at the heart:	A seemingly good apple can be rotten at the core,
O, what a goodly outside falsehood hath!	A seemingly honest appearance can hide lies!

SHYLOCK
Three thousand ducats; 'tis a good round sum.	Three thousand ducats. That's a good round amount.
Three months from twelve; then, let me see; the rate—	Three months out of twelve, well, let me see. The rate—

ANTONIO
Well, Shylock, shall we be beholding to you?	Well, Shylock, will you lend us the money?

SHYLOCK
Signior Antonio, many a time and oft	Signior Antonio, you have often, many times,
In the Rialto you have rated me	Judged my behavior in the Rialto
About my moneys and my usances:	Regarding how I use my money to earn interest.
Still have I borne it with a patient shrug,	I have taken all of this with great patience,
For sufferance is the badge of all our tribe.	For suffering is just what Jews do.
You call me misbeliever, cut-throat dog,	You call me a heretic, a murderous dog,

Original	Modern
And spit upon my Jewish gaberdine,	And spit upon my Jewish cloak.
And all for use of that which is mine own.	All because I'm doing what I want with what is mine.
Well then, it now appears you need my help:	And, well, now it seems you need my help.
Go to, then; you come to me, and you say	All right, then. So, you come to me and you say
'Shylock, we would have moneys:' you say so;	'Shylock, we need some money.' You ask me for it.
You, that did void your rheum upon my beard	You, who spit on my beard
And foot me as you spurn a stranger cur	And kicked me just like you would kick a stray dog out the door.
Over your threshold: moneys is your suit	Here you are now asking for money.
What should I say to you? Should I not say	
'Hath a dog money? is it possible	
A cur can lend three thousand ducats?' Or	
Shall I bend low and in a bondman's key,	So, should I bow to you and in a slave-like tone,
With bated breath and whispering humbleness,	Holding my breath and whispering humbly, say
Say this;	
'Fair sir, you spit on me on Wednesday last;	'Oh, good sir, you spit on me last Wednesday
You spurn'd me such a day; another time	and scorned me another day and another time
You call'd me dog; and for these courtesies	called me a dog, and because of these gestures of respect
I'll lend you thus much moneys'?	I'll lend you as much money as you need?'

ANTONIO
I am as like to call thee so again,	I'm likely to call you a dog again,
To spit on thee again, to spurn thee too.	And to spit on you again, and to scorn you, too.
If thou wilt lend this money, lend it not	If you lend us the money, don't lend it
As to thy friends; for when did friendship take	Like you would to friends. For since when do friends
A breed for barren metal of his friend?	Expect the coins of his friend to reproduce for him?
But lend it rather to thine enemy,	Instead, lend it as if you were lending it to an enemy,
Who, if he break, thou mayst with better face	who—if he goes broke—you can more easily
Exact the penalty.	punish.

SHYLOCK
Why, look you, how you storm!	Well, look at how upset you are getting!
I would be friends with you and have your love,	I want to be friends with you and get along.
Forget the shames that you have stain'd me with,	I can forget all of the shameful things you've done to me
Supply your present wants and take no doit	And lend you the money without taking

Original	Modern
Of usance for my moneys, and you'll not hear me: / This is kind I offer.	interest for the use of it. But you'll not hear / This kind offer I make.

BASSANIO

This were kindness.	It would be kind.

SHYLOCK

This kindness will I show. / Go with me to a notary, seal me there / Your single bond; and, in a merry sport, / If you repay me not on such a day,	I can show this kindness. / Go with me to a notary and let's seal / Your loan without interest. Then, for a joke, / Let's write in that if you don't pay me on a particular day,
In such a place, such sum or sums as are / Express'd in the condition, let the forfeit / Be nominated for an equal pound / Of your fair flesh, to be cut off and taken / In what part of your body pleaseth me.	At a particular location all of the money I lend to you, Let it be said that you will give me / As a penalty an exact pound / Of your flesh, which will be cut off and taken / From whatever part of your body I want.

ANTONIO

Content, i' faith: I'll seal to such a bond / And say there is much kindness in the Jew.	I'll accept that in good faith. I'll sign the bond / And even say that Jews are very kind.

BASSANIO

You shall not seal to such a bond for me: / I'll rather dwell in my necessity.	I will not let you sign such a loan for me. / I'd rather go without the money.

ANTONIO

Why, fear not, man; I will not forfeit it: / Within these two months, that's a month before / This bond expires, I do expect return / Of thrice three times the value of this bond.	Don't worry about it. I won't forfeit it. / Within the next two months, which is a month / Before the amount is due, I expect profits / Of three times the amount of this loan.

SHYLOCK

O father Abram, what these Christians are,	Oh, father Abram, what kind of people these Christians are
Whose own hard dealings teaches them suspect / The thoughts of others! Pray you, tell me this;	Whose own ways of dealing taught them to suspect the intentions of others! Please, just tell me this:
If he should break his day, what should I gain	If he should not have the money on time, what could I possibly gain
By the exaction of the forfeiture? / A pound of man's flesh taken from a man / Is not so estimable, profitable neither, / As flesh of muttons, beefs, or goats. I say,	By taking a pound of his flesh for the forfeit? / A pound of a man's flesh taken from his body / Is not worth very much—it's not even worth as much as the flesh of lambs, cows or goats. I'm

To buy his favour, I extend this friendship:
If he will take it, so; if not, adieu;
And, for my love, I pray you wrong me not.

ANTONIO
Yes Shylock, I will seal unto this bond.

SHYLOCK
Then meet me forthwith at the notary's;
Give him direction for this merry bond,
And I will go and purse the ducats straight,
See to my house, left in the fearful guard
Of an unthrifty knave, and presently
I will be with you.

ANTONIO
Hie thee, gentle Jew.

Exit Shylock
The Hebrew will turn Christian: he grows kind.

BASSANIO
I like not fair terms and a villain's mind.

ANTONIO
Come on: in this there can be no dismay;
My ships come home a month before the day.

Exeunt

---

saying to win his esteem, I am offering this friendship. If he will take it, good. If not, then goodbye. And please don't slander me for making the offer.

Yes, Shylock, I will sign for the loan by your terms.

Then meet me at the notary's
Give him the details of our little joke.
I will go and get the money right away.
First I have to check on my house—I left it under the care of a useless servant. After that I will meet up with you.

Hurry up, my kind Jewish friend.

The Jew is almost Christian, he's being so kind.

I don't like pretty ways from someone with the mind of a villian.

Come on, there's no need to worry.
My ships return a month before the day the loan is due.

Act II

SCENE I. Belmont. A room in PORTIA'S house.

Flourish of cornets. Enter the PRINCE OF MOROCCO and his train; PORTIA, NERISSA, and others attending

MOROCCO
Mislike me not for my complexion,
The shadow'd livery of the burnish'd sun,
To whom I am a neighbour and near bred.
Bring me the fairest creature northward born,

Where Phoebus' fire scarce thaws the icicles,

And let us make incision for your love,
To prove whose blood is reddest, his or mine.
I tell thee, lady, this aspect of mine
Hath fear'd the valiant: by my love I swear
The best-regarded virgins of our clime
Have loved it too: I would not change this hue,
Except to steal your thoughts, my gentle queen.

PORTIA
In terms of choice I am not solely led
By nice direction of a maiden's eyes;

Besides, the lottery of my destiny

Bars me the right of voluntary choosing:
But if my father had not scanted me
And hedged me by his wit, to yield myself

His wife who wins me by that means I told you,
Yourself, renowned prince, then stood as fair

As any comer I have look'd on yet
For my affection.

MOROCCO
Even for that I thank you:
Therefore, I pray you, lead me to the caskets
To try my fortune. By this scimitar
That slew the Sophy and a Persian prince
That won three fields of Sultan Solyman,
I would outstare the sternest eyes that look,

---

*Please don't dislike me for my skin color,
The sun has made my skin so dark
Since I was born under it and lived near it.
Show me the palest skinned man that was born in northern regions,
Where the sun's warmth barely thaws the icicles.
And I will make a cut in my skin
To prove my blood is just as red as his.
I can tell you that the darkness of my skin
Has made brave men fear me and I swear to you the finest young women in my region
Have loved it. I would not change my color
Except to find a place in your thoughts, gentle queen.*

*I am not led in my choice of a husband
Based soley on how good looking a man is to the ladies.
Besides, the contest with the trunks my father devised
Takes away my right to freely choose.
But if my father had not robbed me of chosing, and restricted me with his cleverness, I'd give myself
As wife to any man who wins me fairly,
And you, famous prince, would stand as much a chance
As any other suitor I have already met
Of winning my heart.*

*For that, I thank you.
So, please lead me to the trunks
To try my luck. By this sword
That killed the Sophy and a Persian prince,
That won three battles with Sultan Solyman,
I would outstare the meanest eyes in the world*

Outbrave the heart most daring on the earth,	And act braver than the most daring man on earth.
Pluck the young sucking cubs from the she-bear,	I'd take a mother bear's cubs from her,
Yea, mock the lion when he roars for prey,	And would even tease a roaring, hungry lion
To win thee, lady. But, alas the while!	To win your love, lady. But, this is not good!
If Hercules and Lichas play at dice	If Hercules and Lichas were to toss dice
Which is the better man, the greater throw	To decide which is the better man, the best toss
May turn by fortune from the weaker hand:	May by a turn of luck come from the weaker hand.
So is Alcides beaten by his page;	Just as Alcides could be beaten by his servant,
And so may I, blind fortune leading me,	I might also, led by blind luck,
Miss that which one unworthier may attain,	Miss the opportunity for you that one less worthy might win
And die with grieving.	And I would die with grief about it.

PORTIA
You must take your chance,	You must take your chance,
And either not attempt to choose at all	And either choose not to attempt it at all
Or swear before you choose, if you choose wrong	Or swear before chosing that if you choose wrong
Never to speak to lady afterward	You will never speak to any lady again
In way of marriage: therefore be advised.	About marriage. That's the deal.

MOROCCO
Nor will not. Come, bring me unto my chance.	I won't get married if I lose. So, let me take my chance.

PORTIA
First, forward to the temple: after dinner	Let's go to the temple first. After dinner
Your hazard shall be made.	You can make your guess.

MOROCCO
Good fortune then!	I'll hope for good fortune!
To make me blest or cursed'st among men.	I will be the luckiest man or the most cursed man in the world.

Cornets, and exeunt

SCENE II. Venice. A street.

Enter LAUNCELOT

LAUNCELOT

Certainly my conscience will serve me to run from this Jew my master. The fiend is at mine elbow and	I'm certain I will feel guilty if I run away from this Jew who is my master. But the devil is at my side and
tempts me saying to me 'Gobbo, Launcelot Gobbo, good Launcelot,' or 'good Gobbo,' or good Launcelot	tempts me by saying 'Gobbo, Launcelot Gobbo, good Launcelot,' or 'good Gobbo,' or 'good Launcelot
Gobbo, use your legs, take the start, run away. My conscience says 'No; take heed,' honest Launcelot; take heed, honest Gobbo, or, as aforesaid, 'honest Launcelot Gobbo; do not run;	Gobbo, use your legs and take off and run away.' My conscience says, 'No, be careful,' honest Launcelot, be careful, honest Gobbo, or, as I said before, 'honest Launcelot Gobbo, do not run,
scorn running with thy heels.' Well, the most courageous fiend bids me	hold your heels.' But, not to be deterred, the devil tells me
pack: 'Via!' says the fiend; 'away!' says the	to pack it up. 'Hurry up!' says the devil. 'Let's go!' says the
fiend; 'for the heavens, rouse up a brave mind,' says the fiend, 'and run.' Well, my conscience, hanging about the neck of my heart, says very wisely	devil. 'For God's sake, be brave,' says the devil, 'and run.' Well, my conscience, which hangs close to my heart, says very wisely
to me 'My honest friend Launcelot, being an honest	to me, 'My honest friend Launcelot, you are an honest
man's son,' or rather an honest woman's son; for,	man's son.' Or, rather, an honest woman's son, for
indeed, my father did something smack, something grow to, he had a kind of taste; well, my conscience	my father had characteristics, something that was a part of him, a certain kind of taste for cheating. But my conscience
says 'Launcelot, budge not.' 'Budge,' says the fiend. 'Budge not,' says my conscience. 'Conscience,' say I, 'you counsel well;' ' Fiend,'	says, 'Launcelot, don't run.' 'Run,' says the devil. 'Don't run,' says my conscience. 'Conscience,' I say, 'you give good advice. 'Devil,'
say I, 'you counsel well:' to be ruled by my conscience, I should stay with the Jew my master, who, God bless the mark, is a kind of devil; and, to run away from the Jew, I should be ruled by the fiend, who, saving your reverence, is the devil himself. Certainly the Jew is the very devil	I say, 'you give good advice.' If I go with my conscience, I will stay with my master the Jew, who, to be sure, is a kind of devil. And to run away from the Jew, I will be ruled by the devil, who, forgive me, is the devil himself. Certainly, the Jew is the devil

incarnal; and, in my conscience, my conscience is

but a kind of hard conscience, to offer to counsel me to stay with the Jew. The fiend gives the more friendly counsel: I will run, fiend; my heels are at your command; I will run.

Enter Old GOBBO, with a basket

GOBBO
Master young man, you, I pray you,
which is the way to master Jew's?

LAUNCELOT
[Aside]
O heavens, this is my true-begotten father!
who, being more than sand-blind,
high-gravel blind,
knows me not: I will try confusions with him.

GOBBO
Master young man, you, I pray you,
which is the way to master Jew's?

LAUNCELOT
Turn up on your right hand at the next turning, but, at the next turning of all, on your left; marry, at the very next turning, turn of no hand, but turn down indirectly to the Jew's house.

GOBBO
By God's sonties, 'twill be a hard way to hit. Can you tell me whether one Launcelot,
that dwells with him, dwell with him or no?

LAUNCELOT
Talk you of young Master Launcelot?

[Aside]
Mark me now; now will I raise the waters.

Talk you of young Master Launcelot?

GOBBO

---

incarnate, and in my conscience, I know my conscience is giving me some hard advice to tell me to stay with the Jew. The devil gives kinder advice: I will run, devil, my heels are at your command, I will run.

Can you tell me, young man, please, which is the way the master Jew's home?

[Aside]
Oh my god, it is my real father! And he's more than just a little blind, he's almost totally blind and doesn't recognize me. I'll mess with him a bit.

Can you tell me, young man, please, which is the way the master Jew's home?

Turn right at the next turn, and then turn left. Immediately, at the next turn, turn neither left nor right, but turn in the direction of the Jew's house.

My god, it will be hard to find it. Can you tell me whether a man named Launcelot that used to live there still lives there?

Do you mean the young Master Launcelot?

[Aside] Pay attention, I'm about to make things interesting.
Are you talking about the young Master Launcelot?

No master, sir, but a poor man's son: his father, though I say it, is an honest exceeding poor man and, God be thanked, well to live.	He's not a master, but a poor man's son. His father, if I might say, is an very honest but poor man and—thank God—will most likely live long.
LAUNCELOT Well, let his father be what a' will, we talk of young Master Launcelot.	Well, let his father be what he will, we are talking about young Master Launcelot.
GOBBO Your worship's friend and Launcelot, sir.	I beg your pardon but he is just Launcelot, sir.
LAUNCELOT But I pray you, ergo, old man, ergo, I beseech you, talk you of young Master Launcelot?	But I beg you, therefore, old man, I ask you are you talking about young Master Launcelot?
GOBBO Of Launcelot, an't please your mastership.	I'm talking about Launcelot, yes.
LAUNCELOT Ergo, Master Launcelot. Talk not of Master Launcelot, father; for the young gentleman, according to Fates and Destinies and such odd sayings, the Sisters Three and such branches of learning, is indeed deceased, or, as you would say in plain terms, gone to heaven.	Well, then, Master Launcelot. Don't speak of Master Launcelot, old man, for the young man, according to fate and destiny and other odd reflections, the Three Sisters and those sort of branches of learning, is deceased, or, as one might say in plain terms, he has gone to heaven.
GOBBO Marry, God forbid! the boy was the very staff of my age, my very prop.	By Mary, God forbid! The boy was the very support of my age, he was my prop.
LAUNCELOT Do I look like a cudgel or a hovel-post, a staff or a prop? Do you know me, father?	Do I look like a short stick or a cane, a staff or a prop? Do you know who I am, old man?
GOBBO Alack the day, I know you not, young gentleman: but, I pray you, tell me, is my boy, God rest his soul, alive or dead?	I'm sorry, I do not know who you are, young man, but, please, can you tell me, is my son, God rest his soul, alive or dead?
LAUNCELOT Do you not know me, father?	You don't know me, old man?

GOBBO
Alack, sir, I am sand-blind; I know you not.

LAUNCELOT
Nay, indeed, if you had your eyes,
you might fail of the knowing me:
it is a wise father that knows his
own child. Well, old man, I will tell you news of
your son: give me your blessing: truth will come
to light; murder cannot be hid long; a man's son

may, but at the length truth will out.

GOBBO
Pray you, sir, stand up: I am sure you are not
Launcelot, my boy.

LAUNCELOT
Pray you, let's have no more fooling about it, but

give me your blessing: I am Launcelot, your boy
that was, your son that is, your child that shall
be.

GOBBO
I cannot think you are my son.

LAUNCELOT
I know not what I shall think of that: but I am
Launcelot, the Jew's man,
and I am sure Margery your
wife is my mother.

GOBBO
Her name is Margery, indeed:
I'll be sworn, if thou
be Launcelot, thou art mine own flesh and blood.
Lord worshipped might he be!
what a beard hast thou
got! thou hast got more hair on thy chin than
Dobbin my fill-horse has on his tail.

LAUNCELOT

I'm sorry, sir, I am mostly blind. I do not know you.

No, I think even if you had your sight you wouldn't know me. It is a wise father who can recognize his own child. Well, old man, I will tell you about your son: give me your blessing and the truth will be revelaed. A murder cannot be hidden for long. A man's son may be hidden, but eventually the truth will come out.

Please, sir, stand up. I am sure you are not Launcelot, my son.

Please, let's not have any more fooling around, just give me your blessing. I am Launcelot, your boy that was, your son that is, your child that will always be.

I just can't believe you are my son.

I don't know what to think of that, but I am Launcelot, the Jew's servant, and I am sure that Margery, your wife, is my mother.

Her name is Margery, yes. I'll be damned, if you are Launcelot, you are my flesh and blood. Praise be to God! What a beard you have got! You have more hair on your chin than my draught horse Dobbin has on his tail.

It should seem, then, that Dobbin's tail grows backward: I am sure he had more hair of his tail than I have of my face when I last saw him.

GOBBO
Lord, how art thou changed! How dost thou and thy master agree? I have brought him a present.

How 'gree you now?

LAUNCELOT
Well, well: but, for mine own part, as I have set up my rest to run away, so I will not rest till I have run some ground.
My master's a very Jew: give him a present! give him a halter: I am famished in his service; you may tell every finger I have with my ribs. Father, I am glad you are come: give me your present to one Master Bassanio, who, indeed, gives rare new liveries: if I serve not him, I will run as far as God has any ground. O rare fortune! here comes the man: to him, father; for I am a Jew, if I serve the Jew any longer.

Enter BASSANIO, with LEONARDO and other followers

BASSANIO
You may do so; but let it be so hasted that supper be ready at the farthest by five of the clock. See these letters delivered; put the liveries to making, and desire Gratiano to come anon to my lodging.

Exit a Servant

LAUNCELOT
To him, father.

GOBBO

It would seem, then that Dobbin's tail grows backward. I am sure he had more hair on his tail than I have on my face last time I saw him.

God, how you have changed! How do you and your master get along? I've brought him a present.
How are you these days?

Well, to be honest, as far as I go, I have made up my mind to run away, and I will not rest until I have gained some ground. My master is a Jew. Give him a present! You should give him a noose. I am starving in his service. You can feel every single one of my ribs. Father, I am glad you have come. Give me your present and I will give it to Master Bassanio, who does sometimes give new uniforms. If I can't serve him, I will run as far as God has put ground. Oh, what luck! Here come the man. Let's go talk to him, father. I will be a Jew if I serve a Jew any longer.

Okay, go on. But make sure to do things quickly so that supper is ready no later than five o'clock. Make sure these letters are delivered, and get the uniforms ready, and ask Gratiano to come soon to my home.

Go to him, father.

God bless your worship! | *God bless your, sir!*

BASSANIO
Gramercy! wouldst thou aught with me? | *Thank you! What do you want with me?*

GOBBO
Here's my son, sir, a poor boy,-- | *This is my son, sir, a poor boy—*

LAUNCELOT
Not a poor boy, sir, but the rich Jew's man; that would, sir, as my father shall specify— | *Not a poor boy, sir, but the rich Jew's servant, who would, son, as my father will explain—*

GOBBO
He hath a great infection, sir, as one would say, to serve— | *He very much wants, sir, as one would say, to serve—*

LAUNCELOT
Indeed, the short and the long is, I serve the Jew, and have a desire, as my father shall specify— | *Yes, the short and long of it is that I serve the Jew, and I have a desire, as my father will explain—*

GOBBO
His master and he, saving your worship's reverence, are scarce cater-cousins— | *His master and he are, with all respect to you, are hardly good friends—*

LAUNCELOT
To be brief, the very truth is that the Jew, having done me wrong, doth cause me,
as my father, being, I
hope, an old man, shall frutify unto you— | *To be brief, the truth is that the Jew, having done me wrong, have caused me,
and my father, being, I
hope, an old man, will certify for you—*

GOBBO
I have here a dish of doves that I would bestow upon your worship, and my suit is— | *I have here a dish of doves that I will give to you, sir, and my request is—*

LAUNCELOT
In very brief, the suit is impertinent to myself, as your worship shall know by this honest old man; and, though I say it, though old man,
yet poor man, my father. | *In brief, the request is beside the point, as you, sir, will know by this honest old man, and though I say it, though old,
yet poor, my father.*

BASSANIO
One speak for both. What would you? | *Just one of you speak. What do you want?*

LAUNCELOT

Serve you, sir.

| I want to work for you, sir.

GOBBO
That is the very defect of the matter, sir.

| That is the heart of the matter, sir.

BASSANIO
I know thee well; thou hast obtain'd thy suit:

| I know who you are. You can have whatever you ask.

Shylock thy master spoke with me this day,
And hath preferr'd thee, if it be preferment
To leave a rich Jew's service, to become
The follower of so poor a gentleman.

| Your master Shylock spoke with me today
| And he has recommended you, if you prefer
| To leave a rich Jew's service to become
| The servant of a poor gentleman like me.

LAUNCELOT
The old proverb is very well parted between my master Shylock and you, sir: you have the grace of

| A familiar old proverb is well split between my master Shylock and you, sir. You have the grace of

God, sir, and he hath enough.

| God, and he has enough.

BASSANIO
Thou speak'st it well. Go, father, with thy son.
Take leave of thy old master and inquire
My lodging out. Give him a livery
More guarded than his fellows': see it done.

| Very well said. Go father, with your son
| And take leave of your old master and find
| Your way to my house. Give him a uniform
| More tricked out than the others. See that it's done.

LAUNCELOT
Father, in. I cannot get a service, no; I have

| Father, go ahead. I can't get employment, no. I am not

ne'er a tongue in my head. Well, if any man in

| able to talk my way into it. But I doubt any man in

Italy have a fairer table which doth offer to swear

| Italy has a better palm than I have to swear upon

upon a book, I shall have good fortune. Go to, here's a simple line of life: here's a small trifle

| a Bible, and I will have good luck. Look here, here's a simple line of my life, here's a small amount

of wives: alas, fifteen wives is nothing! eleven

| of wives: I'm sorry, fifteen wives is nothing! Eleven

widows and nine maids is a simple coming-in for one

| widows and nine maids is a simple yield for one

man: and then to 'scape drowning thrice, and to be

| man: and to escape drowning twice, and to have

in peril of my life with the edge of a feather-bed;

| my life in danger because I am found in the wrong bed—

here are simple scapes. Well, if Fortune be a

| these are simple escapes. Well, if Fortune is a

woman, she's a good wench for this gear.
Father, come; I'll take my leave of the Jew in the twinkling of an eye.

Exeunt Launcelot and Old Gobbo

BASSANIO
I pray thee, good Leonardo, think on this:
These things being bought and orderly bestow'd,

Return in haste, for I do feast to-night
My best-esteem'd acquaintance: hie thee, go.

LEONARDO
My best endeavours shall be done herein.

Enter GRATIANO

GRATIANO
Where is your master?

LEONARDO
Yonder, sir, he walks.

Exit

GRATIANO
Signior Bassanio!

BASSANIO
Gratiano!

GRATIANO
I have a suit to you.

BASSANIO
You have obtain'd it.

GRATIANO
You must not deny me:
I must go with you to Belmont.

BASSANIO

woman, she's a good wench for this gear. Father, come; I'll take my leave of the Jew in the twinkling of an eye.	woman, she's a good girl to give me this stuff. Father, come, I'll leave my Jew in the blink of an eye.
I pray thee, good Leonardo, think on this: These things being bought and orderly bestow'd,	Please, good Leonardo, think about this: These are the things to be bought and stored away.
Return in haste, for I do feast to-night My best-esteem'd acquaintance: hie thee, go.	Hurry back, I'm having dinner tonight with someone very important. Hurry up, go.
My best endeavours shall be done herein.	I'll do my best with this.
Where is your master?	Where is your master?
Yonder, sir, he walks.	He's walking over there.
Signior Bassanio!	Signior Bassanio!
Gratiano!	Gratiano!
I have a suit to you.	I have a favor to ask you.
You have obtain'd it.	It's yours.
You must not deny me: I must go with you to Belmont.	You must not say no. I must go with you to Belmont.

Why then you must. But hear thee, Gratiano;	Well, then you must come. But listen to me, Gratiano.
Thou art too wild, too rude and bold of voice;	Sometimes you are wild—too rude and loud.
Parts that become thee happily enough	These things look good on you
And in such eyes as ours appear not faults;	And do not appear to be faults in my eyes.
But where thou art not known, why, there they show	But where people do not know you, well, those things might see,
Something too liberal. Pray thee, take pain	a bit too unrestrained. So, please, take care
To allay with some cold drops of modesty	To lessen that a bit and add some modesty
Thy skipping spirit, lest through thy wild behavior	To your boisterous spirit, to make sure your wild behavior
I be misconstrued in the place I go to,	does not reflect badly on me in Belmont
And lose my hopes.	and cause me to lose hope of winning Portia.

GRATIANO
Signior Bassanio, hear me:	Listen to me, Signior Bassanio:
If I do not put on a sober habit,	If I do not act sober and serious,
Talk with respect and swear but now and then,	And talk with respect and only swear occasionally,
Wear prayer-books in my pocket, look demurely,	Carry a prayer book with me and appear gentle,
Nay more, while grace is saying, hood mine eyes	Even more—if while grace is being said I and I do not cover my eyes
Thus with my hat, and sigh and say 'amen,'	With the brim of my hat and quietly say 'amen,'
Use all the observance of civility,	And act civil and polite at all times,
Like one well studied in a sad ostent	Like someone deliberately putting on a serious display of manners
To please his grandam, never trust me more.	To please his grandmother, then never trust me again.

BASSANIO
Well, we shall see your bearing.	Well, we'll see how you are.

GRATIANO
Nay, but I bar to-night: you shall not gauge me	But tonight doesn't count. Don't judge how I
By what we do to-night.	will be by how I am tonight.

BASSANIO
No, that were pity:	No, that would be a shame.
I would entreat you rather to put on	I would rather you be
Your boldest suit of mirth, for we have friends	As wild as you can be tonight because our
That purpose merriment. But fare you well:	friends will enjoy that and want to have fun. Goodbye for now,
I have some business.	I have some things I have to do.

GRATIANO
And I must to Lorenzo and the rest:

But we will visit you at supper-time.

Exeunt

And I must get back to Lorenzo and the rest of them.
We will see you at dinner.

SCENE III. The same. A room in SHYLOCK'S house.

Enter JESSICA and LAUNCELOT

JESSICA
I am sorry thou wilt leave my father so:
Our house is hell, and thou, a merry devil,
Didst rob it of some taste of tediousness.
But fare thee well, there is a ducat for thee:
And, Launcelot, soon at supper shalt thou see
Lorenzo, who is thy new master's guest:
Give him this letter; do it secretly;
And so farewell: I would not have my father
See me in talk with thee.

I'm sorry you are leaving my father's service: This house is hellish and you cheered it up like a funny devil, taking away some small amount of the pain of it all. But, goodbye and take care, here is a ducat for you: Lorenzo, who will be your new master's guest tonight— Please give him this letter. Do it secretly. Well, goodbye. I don't want my Father to see me talking to you.

LAUNCELOT
Adieu! tears exhibit my tongue. Most beautiful
pagan, most sweet Jew! if a Christian did not play
the knave and get thee, I am much deceived. But,
adieu: these foolish drops do something drown my
manly spirit: adieu.

Goodbye! My tears show what I cannot say. Most beautiful pagan, most sweet Jew! A Christian will figure out a way to get you, I have no doubt. But goodbye: these foolish tears don't do much to make me appear manly: goodbye.

JESSICA
Farewell, good Launcelot.

Goodbye, good Launcelot.

Exit Launcelot

Alack, what heinous sin is it in me
To be ashamed to be my father's child!
But though I am a daughter to his blood,
I am not to his manners. O Lorenzo,
If thou keep promise, I shall end this strife,
Become a Christian and thy loving wife.

Oh my god, how terrible am I To be ashamed to be my father's daughter! But though I am his daughter by blood, I do not share his behavior. Oh, Lorenzo, If you keep your promise, this will all end And I'll become a Christian and your loving wife.

Exit

SCENE IV. The same. A street.

Enter GRATIANO, LORENZO, SALARINO, and SALANIO

LORENZO
Nay, we will slink away in supper-time,
Disguise us at my lodging and return,
All in an hour.

> No, we'll sneak away at dinner time,
> Disguise ourselves at my house and come back within an hour.

GRATIANO
We have not made good preparation.

> But we don't have anything ready.

SALARINO
We have not spoke us yet of torchbearers.

> We haven't even asked anyone to be torchbearers.

SALANIO
'Tis vile, unless it may be quaintly order'd,
And better in my mind not undertook.

> It might turn out badly since it's not well organized. I think it's best we call it off.

LORENZO
'Tis now but four o'clock: we have two hours
To furnish us.

> It's only four o'clock now: we have two hours to get it together.

Enter LAUNCELOT, with a letter

Friend Launcelot, what's the news?

> Hello, Launcelot, what's up?

LAUNCELOT
An it shall please you to break up
this, it shall seem to signify.

> Here, if you'd like to open this letter, it will give you the news.

LORENZO
I know the hand: in faith, 'tis a fair hand;

> I recognize the handwriting, no doubt. It's beautiful handwriting.

And whiter than the paper it writ on
Is the fair hand that writ.

> And as white as the paper this writing is on, the beautiful hand that wrote it is whiter.

GRATIANO
Love-news, in faith.

> I believe it's a love letter.

LAUNCELOT
By your leave, sir.

> May I go, sir?

LORENZO

Original	Modern
Whither goest thou?	Where are you going?
LAUNCELOT	
Marry, sir, to bid my old master the Jew to sup to-night with my new master the Christian.	Sir, I have to go invite my old master the Jew to join tonight with my new master the Christian.
LORENZO	
Hold here, take this: tell gentle Jessica I will not fail her; speak it privately. Go, gentlemen,	Hold on, take this: tell gentle Jessica I will not fail her. Tell her privately. Go on, gentlemen—
Exit Launcelot	
Will you prepare you for this masque tonight? I am provided of a torch-bearer.	Get ready for the masquerade tonight. I have someone who can be a torch-bearer.
SALANIO	
Ay, marry, I'll be gone about it straight.	Okay, I'll go ahead and get right on it.
SALANIO	
And so will I.	So will I.
LORENZO	
Meet me and Gratiano At Gratiano's lodging some hour hence.	Meet me and Gratiano At Gratiano's house in an hour.
SALARINO	
'Tis good we do so.	It's good we're doing this.
Exeunt SALARINO and SALANIO	
GRATIANO	
Was not that letter from fair Jessica?	Wan't that letter from Jessica?
LORENZO	
I must needs tell thee all. She hath directed How I shall take her from her father's house, What gold and jewels she is furnish'd with, What page's suit she hath in readiness. If e'er the Jew her father come to heaven, It will be for his gentle daughter's sake: And never dare misfortune cross her foot, Unless she do it under this excuse,	I have to tell you everything. She has told me How I can get her out of her father's house, And what gold and jewels she has, She decribed a page's suit she has ready. If the Jew her father ever makes it to heaven, It will be because of her; She'll never suffer from bad luck, Unless it happens because of one reason:

That she is issue to a faithless Jew.

Come, go with me; peruse this as thou goest:
Fair Jessica shall be my torch-bearer.

Exeunt

That she is the daughter of an unbeleiving Jew.
Come on, go with me. Read this as we go.
Beautiful Jessica is going to be my torch-bearer.

SCENE V. The same. Before SHYLOCK'S house.

Enter SHYLOCK and LAUNCELOT

SHYLOCK
Well, thou shalt see, thy eyes shall be thy judge,

The difference of old Shylock and Bassanio:--

What, Jessica!--thou shalt not gormandise,
As thou hast done with me:--What, Jessica!--
And sleep and snore, and rend apparel out;--
Why, Jessica, I say!

LAUNCELOT
Why, Jessica!

SHYLOCK
Who bids thee call? I do not bid thee call.

LAUNCELOT
Your worship was wont to tell me that
I could do nothing without bidding.

Enter Jessica

JESSICA
Call you? what is your will?

SHYLOCK
I am bid forth to supper, Jessica:
There are my keys. But wherefore should I go?
I am not bid for love; they flatter me:

But yet I'll go in hate, to feed upon
The prodigal Christian. Jessica, my girl,
Look to my house. I am right loath to go:
There is some ill a-brewing towards my rest,

For I did dream of money-bags to-night.

LAUNCELOT
I beseech you, sir, go:
my young master doth expect

Well, you'll see how it is—you'll see it with your own eyes,
The difference between working for old Shylock and Bassanio—
Jessica!—you will not eat so greedily
As you have done here—Jessica!—
And sleep and snore, and wear your cloths out— Jessica, come here, I'm calling you!

Jessica!

Why do you call her? I didn't tell you to call her.

You always told me
I couldn't do anything unless you said I could.

Did you call? What do you want?

I am invited for dinner, Jessica,
Here are my keys/ But why should I go?
The invite is not because they like me. They're just flattering me.
But I'll go out of spite, to feast at the expense of the wasteful Christian. Jessica, my girl,
Look after the house. I am hesitant to go:
There's something up that is making me uneasy.
I know because I dreamt of money bags last night.

Please, sir, go.
My new master is expecting

your reproach. SHYLOCK So do I his.	you to approach. And I expect his reproach.
LAUNCELOT And they have conspired together, I will not say you shall see a masque; but if you do, then it was not for nothing that my nose fell a-bleeding on Black-Monday last at six o'clock i' the morning, falling out that year on Ash-Wednesday was four year, in the afternoon.	And they have been making plans. I will not say you will see a masquerade, but if you do, then it wasn't for nothing that my nose started bleeding on this past Easter Monday at six o'clock in the morning, exactly like it did on Ash Wednesday four years ago in the afternoon.
SHYLOCK What, are there masques? Hear you me, Jessica: Lock up my doors; and when you hear the drum And the vile squealing of the wry-neck'd fife, Clamber not you up to the casements then, Nor thrust your head into the public street To gaze on Christian fools with varnish'd faces, But stop my house's ears, I mean my casements: Let not the sound of shallow foppery enter My sober house. By Jacob's staff, I swear, I have no mind of feasting forth to-night: But I will go. Go you before me, sirrah; Say I will come.	What, there's going to be a masquerade? Listen to me, Jessica: Lock up my doors and when you hear the drum And the disgusting squealing of the crooked flute Don't crawl up to the windows Or stick your head out to look into the street To look at the Christrian fools with painted faces, Instead, plug up my house's ears, I mean my windows; Don't let the sound of shallow foolishness enter my serious house. By Jacob's staff, I swear, I'm not in the mood to go out feasting tonight, But I will go. Go on ahead of me, then, And tell them I will come.
LAUNCELOT I will go before, sir. Mistress, look out at window, for all this, There will come a Christian boy, will be worth a Jewess' eye.	I will go ahead, sir. Mistress, look out the window later, and you will see the arrival of a Christian boy well worth the glance of a Jewess' eye.

Exit

SHYLOCK

What says that fool of Hagar's offspring, ha?

JESSICA
His words were 'Farewell mistress;' nothing else.

SHYLOCK
The patch is kind enough, but a huge feeder;
Snail-slow in profit, and he sleeps by day

More than the wild-cat: drones hive not with me;

Therefore I part with him, and part with him
To one that would have him help to waste
His borrow'd purse. Well, Jessica, go in;

Perhaps I will return immediately:
Do as I bid you; shut doors after you:

Fast bind, fast find;

A proverb never stale in thrifty mind.

Exit

JESSICA
Farewell; and if my fortune be not crost,
I have a father, you a daughter, lost.

Exit

What did that fool say to you, huh?

He said 'Goodbye mistress,' and nothing else.

*The fool is nice enough, but he eats a lot.
He is slow as a snail when he works, and he naps
As much as a cat. Bees that don't work can't stay in my hive
So I am letting him go, and letting him work
For the one that will have help to waste
The money he borrowed from me. Well, Jessica, go inside.
I may very well return immediately.
Do as I tell you and shut the doors behind you.
Lock things up and you will find them where you left them,
Which is a saying that is always fresh in a thrifty mind.*

*Goodbye, and if my luck holds out,
I will lose a father and you will lose a daughter.*

SCENE VI. The same.

Enter GRATIANO and SALARINO, masque

GRATIANO
This is the pent-house under which Lorenzo
Desired us to make stand.

| | This is the roof that Lorenzo wants us to wait under. |

SALARINO
His hour is almost past.

| | It's after the time he said he'd be here. |

GRATIANO
And it is marvel he out-dwells his hour,
For lovers ever run before the clock.

| | It is surprising that he is late Because lovers are usually early. |

SALARINO
O, ten times faster Venus' pigeons fly
To seal love's bonds new-made, than they are wont
To keep obliged faith unforfeited!

| | Yes, time flies ten times faster for those who are newly in love that it does for those who have been married a long time and are trying to remain faithful! |

GRATIANO
That ever holds: who riseth from a feast

With that keen appetite that he sits down?

Where is the horse that doth untread again
His tedious measures with the unbated fire

That he did pace them first? All things that are,
Are with more spirit chased than enjoy'd.

How like a younker or a prodigal

The scarfed bark puts from her native bay,
Hugg'd and embraced by the strumpet wind!
How like the prodigal doth she return,
With over-weather'd ribs and ragged sails,
Lean, rent and beggar'd by the strumpet wind!

| | That's the case for a lot of things: who rises from a feast With the same sharp appetite as when he sat down? Where is a horse that can retrace again His careful footsteps with the same intense heat with which He first ran them? All the things we want Are chased after with more enthusiasm than they are enjoyed. Just like a fashionable young man or a favorite son— A fully decked out ship leaves her bay, Lovingly embraced by the wind, But like the prodigal son she returns, With weather worn ribs and ragged sails, Made lean, torn and destitute by the same wind. |

SALARINO
Here comes Lorenzo: more of this hereafter.

| | Here comes Lorenzo. We can talk more about this later. |

Enter LORENZO

LORENZO Sweet friends, your patience for my long abode;	My good friends, thanks for your patience with my delay.
Not I, but my affairs, have made you wait:	It wasn't me, but my business, that made me late.
When you shall please to play the thieves for wives,	When you, too, have to be thieves to get your wives,
I'll watch as long for you then. Approach; Here dwells my father Jew. Ho! who's within?	I'll wait as long for you, then. Come here. This is the house of my future father-in-law. Hello! Who's inside?

Enter JESSICA, above, in boy's clothes

JESSICA Who are you? Tell me, for more certainty, Albeit I'll swear that I do know your tongue.	Who are you? Tell me, so I can be certain, Although I swear I know you by your voice.
LORENZO Lorenzo, and thy love.	It's Lorenzo, your love.
JESSICA Lorenzo, certain, and my love indeed, For who love I so much? And now who knows But you, Lorenzo, whether I am yours?	Lorenzo, for certain, and my love for sure. Who else do I love so much? Who knows now but you, Lorenzo, whether I am yours?
LORENZO Heaven and thy thoughts are witness that thou art.	As God is my witness, you know you are mine.
JESSICA Here, catch this casket; it is worth the pains.	Here, catch this box—it will be worth the trouble.
I am glad 'tis night, you do not look on me, For I am much ashamed of my exchange: But love is blind and lovers cannot see The pretty follies that themselves commit; For if they could, Cupid himself would blush To see me thus transformed to a boy.	I am glad it is dark and you can not see me Because I am ashamed of my appearance. But love is blind and lovers cannot see The silly things they do. If they could, Cupid himself would blush To see me transformed into a boy.
LORENZO Descend, for you must be my torchbearer.	Come down because you are to be my torchbearer.
JESSICA What, must I hold a candle to my shames? They in themselves, good-sooth, are too too light.	Really, I have to hold a light to my disgrace? My disguise is, in fact, itself a bit sleazy.

Why, 'tis an office of discovery, love;
And I should be obscured.

LORENZO
So are you, sweet,
Even in the lovely garnish of a boy.
But come at once;
For the close night doth play the runaway,
And we are stay'd for at Bassanio's feast.

JESSICA
I will make fast the doors, and gild myself
With some more ducats, and be with you straight.

Exit above

GRATIANO
Now, by my hood, a Gentile and no Jew.

LORENZO
Beshrew me but I love her heartily;
For she is wise, if I can judge of her,
And fair she is, if that mine eyes be true,
And true she is, as she hath proved herself,
And therefore, like herself, wise, fair and true,

Shall she be placed in my constant soul.

Enter JESSICA, below

What, art thou come? On, gentlemen; away!

Our masquing mates by this time for us stay.

Exit with Jessica and Salarino
Enter ANTONIO

ANTONIO
Who's there?

GRATIANO
Signior Antonio!

ANTONIO

The light will serve
What really shoul...

You are still sw...
Even when yo...
Come on, let...
The night is pass...
And we are late for Bass...

I will lock the doors and grab
Some more money and be right down.

I think she acts more than a Gentile than a Jew.

Damn, but I love her like crazy!
She is wise, if I'm observing correctly,
And beautiful, if my eyes see right.
And she is loyal, and has proven that.
And with her being so wise, beautiful and faithful,
She will have a place in my heart forever.

Well, you've finally come down? Let's go, gentlemen!
Our mascarading friends are waiting for us.

Who's there?

Signior Antonio!

Fie, fie, Gratia...
'Tis nine o'c...
No maso...
Bass...
I b...

...no! where are all the rest?
...ock: our friends all stay for you.
...ue to-night: the wind is come about;
...anio presently will go aboard:
...ave sent twenty out to seek for you.

GRATIANO
I am glad on't: I desire no more delight
Than to be under sail and gone to-night.

Exeunt

*Gratiano! Where is everybody?
It's nine o'clock—our friends are waiting for you.
There won't be a masquerade tonight. The wind has turned direction,
And Bassianio wants to ship out tonight.
I've got twenty men out looking for you.*

I'm glad to hear it. I can't think of anything more I'd rather do than to leave tonight.

SCENE VII. Belmont. A room in PORTIA'S house.

Flourish of cornets. Enter PORTIA, with the PRINCE OF MOROCCO, and their trains

PORTIA Go draw aside the curtains and discover The several caskets to this noble prince. Now make your choice.	Open the curtains to reveal The trunks to this noble prince. Now, make your choice.
MOROCCO The first, of gold, who this inscription bears,	The first one is made of gold and it bear this inscription:
'Who chooseth me shall gain what many men desire;' The second, silver, which this promise carries,	'Whoever chooses me will get what many men want.' The second, which is made of silver, bears the promise:
'Who chooseth me shall get as much as he deserves;' This third, dull lead, with warning all as blunt,	'Whoever chooses me will get all that he deserves.' The third, made of dull lead, bears a blunt warning:
'Who chooseth me must give and hazard all he hath.' How shall I know if I do choose the right?	'Whoever chooses me must give and risk all he has.' How can I know which one to choose?
PORTIA The one of them contains my picture, prince: If you choose that, then I am yours withal.	One of them contains my picture, prince. If you choose that one, then I am yours forever, and so is the picture.
MOROCCO Some god direct my judgment! Let me see; I will survey the inscriptions back again. What says this leaden casket? 'Who chooseth me must give and hazard all he hath.' Must give: for what? for lead? hazard for lead?	I need a god to help me decide! Let me see— I will take a look at the inscriptions again. What's it say on this lead trunk? 'Whoever chooses me must give and risk all he has.' Must give all, for what? Lead? Risk all for lead?
This casket threatens. Men that hazard all Do it in hope of fair advantages: A golden mind stoops not to shows of dross;	This trunk seems threatening. Men that risk all Do it in hope of much gain. A golden mind will not stoop to pick up things that look like garbage.
I'll then nor give nor hazard aught for lead. What says the silver with her virgin hue?	I'll then give nothing or risk anything for lead. What does the silver one that is shining like new say?
'Who chooseth me shall get as much as he	'Whoever chooses me will get all that he

deserves.' As much as he deserves! Pause there, Morocco,	deserves.' As much as he deserves! Stop for a moment and think, Morocco.
And weigh thy value with an even hand: If thou be'st rated by thy estimation, Thou dost deserve enough; and yet enough May not extend so far as to the lady: And yet to be afeard of my deserving Were but a weak disabling of myself. As much as I deserve! Why, that's the lady:	And weigh your worth fairly. If you have a good reputaion, You deserve enough, but enough Might not be enough to include this lady. And yet to be afraid of my own worthiness, Would be to underestimate myself. As much as I deserve! Well, I deserve the lady.
I do in birth deserve her, and in fortunes, In graces and in qualities of breeding; But more than these, in love I do deserve.	By birthright I deserve her, and by my wealth, By my talents and my fine upbringing, And even more than all of these, by my love I deserve her.
What if I stray'd no further, but chose here?	What if I didn't consider any further and stopped right here?
Let's see once more this saying graved in gold	Let's look one more time at what the inscription on the gold one says:
'Who chooseth me shall gain what many men desire.' Why, that's the lady; all the world desires her;	'Whoever chooses me will get want many men want.' Why, that's Portia. Every man in the world desires her.
From the four corners of the earth they come,	From all around the world they come to court her,
To kiss this shrine, this mortal-breathing saint:	To kiss this shrine and see this living and breathing saint.
The Hyrcanian deserts and the vasty wilds	Through the Hyrcanian deserts and the vast wilds
Of wide Arabia are as thoroughfares now For princes to come view fair Portia: The watery kingdom, whose ambitious head Spits in the face of heaven, is no bar	Of Arabia with frequency Princes travel just to lay eyes on her. The ocean, with its deep waters And high waves that lift to the sky do not present a barrier
To stop the foreign spirits, but they come, As o'er a brook, to see fair Portia.	To stop the foreigners—they still come, As if simply crossing a brook, to see beautiful Portia.
One of these three contains her heavenly picture.	One of these three trunks contains her beautiful picture.
Is't like that lead contains her? 'Twere damnation	Is it the lead trunk that contains her picture? It would be a sin
To think so base a thought: it were too gross	To even think such a low thought. It would be too gross
To rib her cerecloth in the obscure grave.	To put her image in that grave-like trunk.

Or shall I think in silver she's immured,	Should I think her picture is closed inside the silver trunk,
Being ten times undervalued to tried gold?	Being ten times less in value than the gold?
O sinful thought! Never so rich a gem	Oh, that's a sinful thought! A rich gem such as she
Was set in worse than gold. They have in England	Should never be placed in anything less than gold. In England they have
A coin that bears the figure of an angel	A coin that bears the likeness of an angel
Stamped in gold, but that's insculp'd upon;	Stamped in gold, that's a carving.
But here an angel in a golden bed	In this case, an angel in a golden bed
Lies all within. Deliver me the key:	Lies inside. Give me the key:
Here do I choose, and thrive I as I may!	I make my choice, and will see what happens!

PORTIA
There, take it, prince; and if my form lie there,	Here, take the key, prince, and if my picture is inside,
Then I am yours.	Then I am yours.

He unlocks the golden casket

MOROCCO
O hell! what have we here?	Damn! What is this?
A carrion Death, within whose empty eye	A skull. And placed in its empty eye
There is a written scroll! I'll read the writing.	Is a piece of paper with writing on it. I'll read it.

Reads
All that glitters is not gold;	All that glitters is not gold,
Often have you heard that told:	You've heard that said often.
Many a man his life hath sold	Many men have sold their souls
But my outside to behold:	Just to find a golden surface.
Gilded tombs do worms enfold.	Graves with gold headstones hold worms.
Had you been as wise as bold,	If you have been as wise as you were bold,
Young in limbs, in judgment old,	With an old man's wisdom despite your youth,
Your answer had not been inscroll'd:	You wouldn't be reading this now.
Fare you well; your suit is cold.	Farewell—you made the wrong guess.
Cold, indeed; and labour lost:	Wrong, for sure, and your work is for nothing.
Then, farewell, heat, and welcome, frost!	So, goodbye, desire, and welcome, hopelessness!
Portia, adieu. I have too grieved a heart	Portia, goodbye. My heart is too sad
To take a tedious leave: thus losers part.	too stay any longer. As a loser, I'm leaving.

Exit with his train. Flourish of cornets

PORTIA
A gentle riddance. Draw the curtains, go.	Good riddance. Draw the curtains and leave.

Let all of his complexion choose me so.   *I hope everyone dark like him chooses the same way.*

Exeunt

SCENE VIII. Venice. A street.

Enter SALARINO and SALANIO

SALARINO
Why, man, I saw Bassanio under sail:
With him is Gratiano gone along;
And in their ship I am sure Lorenzo is not.

SALANIO
The villain Jew with outcries raised the duke,
Who went with him to search Bassanio's ship.

SALARINO
He came too late, the ship was under sail:

But there the duke was given to understand

That in a gondola were seen together
Lorenzo and his amorous Jessica:
Besides, Antonio certified the duke
They were not with Bassanio in his ship.

SALANIO
I never heard a passion so confused,
So strange, outrageous, and so variable,
As the dog Jew did utter in the streets:

'My daughter! O my ducats! O my daughter!
Fled with a Christian! O my Christian ducats!

Justice! the law! my ducats, and my daughter!
A sealed bag, two sealed bags of ducats,
Of double ducats, stolen from me by my daughter!

And jewels, two stones, two rich and precious stones,
Stolen by my daughter! Justice! find the girl;
She hath the stones upon her, and the ducats.'

SALARINO
Why, all the boys in Venice follow him,
Crying, his stones, his daughter, and his ducats.

Well, I saw Bassanio sail away
And Gratiano went along with him
I'm sure Lorenzo is not on their ship.

That lowlife Jew complained to the duke
Who went with him to search Bassanio's ship.

He was too late—the ship was already under sail.
When he got there, the duke heard someone say
That a gondola had been spotted
With Lorenzo and his lover Jessica in it.
Besides that, Antonio assured the duke
That Lorenzo and Jessica were not on Bassanio's ship.

I've never heard such a confused outburst—
So startling, unexpected and all over the place
As the way the dog Jew cried out in the streets.

'My daughter! My ducats! My daughter!
Ran away with a Christian! My Christian ducats!

Justice! The law! My ducats and my daughter!
A sealed bag, two sealed bags of ducats,
Of double ducats, stolen from me by my daughter!

And jewels, two jewels, two rich and precious jewels,
Stolen by my daughter! Justice! Find the girl.
She has my jewels and the ducats.'

All the boys in Venice are following him,
Crying 'his stones, his daughter and his ducats.'

SALANIO Let good Antonio look he keep his day, Or he shall pay for this.	*Antonio had better be sure to pay the loan on time, Or he will pay for this.*
SALARINO Marry, well remember'd. I reason'd with a Frenchman yesterday, Who told me, in the narrow seas that part The French and English, there miscarried A vessel of our country richly fraught: I thought upon Antonio when he told me; And wish'd in silence that it were not his.	*Yes, that's a good thing to remember. I was talking with a Frenchman yesterday Who told me that in the narrow sea between France and England, there was a wreck Of a ship from our country full of treasure. I thought about Antonio when I heard this And silently prayed it was not his ship.*
SALANIO You were best to tell Antonio what you hear; Yet do not suddenly, for it may grieve him.	*You should probably tell Antonio what you heard, But do it gently so as not to upset him.*
SALARINO A kinder gentleman treads not the earth. I saw Bassanio and Antonio part: Bassanio told him he would make some speed Of his return: he answer'd, 'Do not so; Slubber not business for my sake, Bassanio But stay the very riping of the time; And for the Jew's bond which he hath of me, Let it not enter in your mind of love: Be merry, and employ your chiefest thoughts To courtship and such fair ostents of love As shall conveniently become you there:' And even there, his eye being big with tears, Turning his face, he put his hand behind him, And with affection wondrous sensible He wrung Bassanio's hand; and so they parted.	*There's not a kinder man on this earth. I saw Bassanio and Antonio saying goodbye: Bassanio told him he would hurry Back and Antonio answered, 'Don't Rush your business for my sake, Bassanio But stay as long as you need to stay. As for the loan that I owe the Jew— Don't even think about it. Be happy and put your mind To wooing your love and the displays of love As will help you to win her while you are there.' And then, with tears in his eyes, He looked away, but he offered his hand And with extraordinary affection He shook Bassanio's hand and they parted.*
SALANIO I think he only loves the world for him. I pray thee, let us go and find him out And quicken his embraced heaviness With some delight or other.	*I think he only loves the world because of Bassanio. How about we go and find him And try to lift his sadness and find a way to cheer him up.*

SALARINO
Do we so. | *Let's do that.*
Exeunt
SCENE IX. Belmont. A room in PORTIA'S house.

Enter NERISSA with a Servitor

NERISSA
Quick, quick, I pray thee; draw the curtain straight: | *Hurry, hurry—draw the curtains right away!*
The Prince of Arragon hath ta'en his oath, | *The Prince of Arragon has sworn in,*
And comes to his election presently. | *and he's coming to make his choice soon.*

Flourish of cornets. Enter the PRINCE OF ARRAGON, PORTIA, and their trains

PORTIA
Behold, there stand the caskets, noble prince: | *Look there—those are the trunks, noble prince.*

If you choose that wherein I am contain'd, | *If you choose the one with my picture in it,*
Straight shall our nuptial rites be solemnized: | *We will be married right away.*
But if you fail, without more speech, my lord, | *But if you fail, you must not say anything more,*

You must be gone from hence immediately. | *And must leave from here immediately.*

ARRAGON
I am enjoin'd by oath to observe three things: | *I am under oath to do three things:*
First, never to unfold to any one | *First, I must never tell anyone*
Which casket 'twas I chose; next, if I fail | *Which trunk it was that I chose. Next, if I fail*
Of the right casket, never in my life | *To pick the right trunk, I must never in my life*
To woo a maid in way of marriage: Lastly, | *Ask a woman to marry me. And last,*
If I do fail in fortune of my choice, | *If I don't make the right choice,*
Immediately to leave you and be gone. | *I must leave immediately.*

PORTIA
To these injunctions every one doth swear | *Everone has to swear to the same orders*
That comes to hazard for my worthless self. | *Who come to take a chance to win me as a prize.*

ARRAGON
And so have I address'd me. Fortune now | *And now I'm ready. May good luck*
To my heart's hope! Gold; silver; and base lead. | *Reward my heart's hope! Gold, silver and lead.*

'Who chooseth me must give and hazard all he hath.' | *'Whoever chooses me must give and risk all that he has.'*
You shall look fairer, ere I give or hazard. | *You'd have to be more beautiful for me to give it all or risk.*

Original	Translation
What says the golden chest? ha! let me see:	Let's see what the golden trunk says. Well! Let me see:
'Who chooseth me shall gain what many men desire.'	'Whoever chooses me will get what many men want.'
What many men desire! that 'many' may be meant	What many men want! By 'many men' it means
By the fool multitude, that choose by show,	The foolish masses who chose by what looks good.
Not learning more than the fond eye doth teach;	And not by figuring out what is there beyond the looks.
Which pries not to the interior, but, like the martlet,	That kind of thinking doesn't look at what's inside, but—like a martin—
Builds in the weather on the outward wall,	Builds its nests exposed on the outside walls,
Even in the force and road of casualty.	Despite possible violence and destruction.
I will not choose what many men desire,	I will not choose what many men want,
Because I will not jump with common spirits	Because I will not jump on the bandwagon
And rank me with the barbarous multitudes.	And go along with what the uncivilized masses want.
Why, then to thee, thou silver treasure-house;	Well, I'm guessing it is the silver trunk.
Tell me once more what title thou dost bear:	Let see again what its inscription says.
'Who chooseth me shall get as much as he deserves:'	'Whoever choses me will get all that he deserves.'
And well said too; for who shall go about	That's well said, for who would expect
To cozen fortune and be honourable	To gain riches and be upright
Without the stamp of merit? Let none presume	Without deserving it? No one should assume
To wear an undeserved dignity.	They should get what they don't deserve.
O, that estates, degrees and offices	If high rank, degrees and offices
Were not derived corruptly, and that clear honour	Were not gained by corruption, but earned with honor
Were purchased by the merit of the wearer!	By the person who gains them!
How many then should cover that stand bare!	How many men would have a position that now do not!
How many be commanded that command!	How many would be commanded that now command!
How much low peasantry would then be glean'd	How many upper ranks would be shown to be peasants
From the true seed of honour! and how much Honour	It rank were based on good name. And how many dignified
Pick'd from the chaff and ruin of the times	Would be picked from the discarded who've been tossed aside
To be new-varnish'd! Well, but to my choice:	To become newly decked out! Well, anyway—regarding my choice:
'Who chooseth me shall get as much as he deserves.'	'Whoever chooses me will get all that he deserves.'

Original	Modern
I will assume desert. Give me a key for this,	I will assume I am deserving. Give me the key for this trunk
And instantly unlock my fortunes here.	and I will unlock it to find my fate.

He opens the silver casket

PORTIA
Too long a pause for that which you find there.

You're taking to long to say what it is you found in there.

ARRAGON
What's here? the portrait of a blinking idiot,
Presenting me a schedule! I will read it.
How much unlike art thou to Portia!
How much unlike my hopes and my deservings!

*What's this? A picture of a blind idiot
Showing me a list! I will read it.
This picture looks nothing like Portia!
This is not what I'd hoped for and it is not what I deserve!*

'Who chooseth me shall have as much as he deserves.'
Did I deserve no more than a fool's head?

*'Whoever chooses me will get all that he deserves.'
Do I not deserve more that a picture of an idiot?*

Is that my prize? are my deserts no better?

Is this my prize? Do I deserve no better?

PORTIA
To offend, and judge, are distinct offices

And of opposed natures.

*Finding offense and judging what you deserve come from places
completely opposite in feeling.*

ARRAGON
What is here?

What is this?

Reads
The fire seven times tried this:
Seven times tried that judgment is,

*This trunk has gone through fire seven times—
Seven times to make sure the person who chooses it*

That did never choose amiss.
Some there be that shadows kiss;
Such have but a shadow's bliss:

*Did not choose it wrongly.
Some will kiss shadows,
And those will have only the happiness shadow's can bring.*

There be fools alive, I wis,
Silver'd o'er; and so was this.

*There are fools alive on this earth, I know,
Who are silver haired the same way as this trunk.*

Take what wife you will to bed,
I will ever be your head:

*Take whatever wife you will,
But you will always have a fool's head like the one in the picture.*

So be gone: you are sped.

So, go away—your work was quick here.

Still more fool I shall appear
By the time I linger here
With one fool's head I came to woo,
But I go away with two.
Sweet, adieu. I'll keep my oath,
Patiently to bear my wroth.

Exeunt Arragon and train
PORTIA
Thus hath the candle singed the moth.
O, these deliberate fools! when they do choose,

They have the wisdom by their wit to lose.

NERISSA
The ancient saying is no heresy,
Hanging and wiving goes by destiny.

PORTIA
Come, draw the curtain, Nerissa.

Enter a Servant

Servant
Where is my lady?

PORTIA
Here: what would my lord?

Servant
Madam, there is alighted at your gate
A young Venetian, one that comes before
To signify the approaching of his lord;
From whom he bringeth sensible regreets,
To wit, besides commends and courteous breath,
Gifts of rich value. Yet I have not seen
So likely an ambassador of love:
A day in April never came so sweet,
To show how costly summer was at hand,
As this fore-spurrer comes before his lord.

PORTIA
No more, I pray thee: I am half afeard
Thou wilt say anon he is some kin to thee,

---

*I will appear more the fool
The longer I stay.
I came here with a fool's head,
But I leave with two.
Goodbye, I will keep my oath
And will calmly endure my misfortune.*

*They were singed like moths to the candle!
Oh, those calculating fools! When they choose,
They have just about enough wisdom to lose.*

*The ancient saying is no lie:
Men die and marry by destiny.*

Please, close the curtain, Nerissa.

Where is my lady?

I'm here—what do you need?

*Madam, there is at your gate
A young Venetian who is coming
Ahead to announce the arrival of his lord,
And he delivers very polite greetings
And—besides the courteous words—
He brings gifts of great value. I have not seen
Such a promising suitor so far.
A day in April could not be so sweet
To show the promise of summer to come
As this messenger shows of his lord.*

*Please, say nothing else. I am almost afraid
You will say he is somehow related to you.*

Thou spend'st such high-day wit in praising him. Come, come, Nerissa; for I long to see Quick Cupid's post that comes so mannerly.	*You put so much energy into praising him. Let's go, Nerissa, I want to see This potential love who has been so well announced.*
NERISSA Bassanio, lord Love, if thy will it be!	*Lord, I so hope it is Bassanio!*

Exeunt

Act III

SCENE I. Venice. A street.

Enter SALANIO and SALARINO

SALANIO
Now, what news on the Rialto?

| | Now what's the news on the Rialto? |

SALARINO
Why, yet it lives there uncheck'd that Antonio hath
a ship of rich lading wrecked on the narrow seas;

the Goodwins, I think they call the place; a very

dangerous flat and fatal, where the carcasses
of many
a tall ship lie buried, as they say, if my gossip
Report be an honest woman of her word.

| | There's a rumor that Antonio had a ship full of treaure wrecked in the English Chanel. on the place called the Goodwins, I think, a very dangerous flat that proves fatal to ships. Many tall ships have sunk there, if the rumors I hear are correct. |

SALANIO
I would she were as lying a gossip in that as ever
knapped ginger or made her neighbours believe she

wept for the death of a third husband. But it is

true, without any slips of prolixity or crossing the
plain highway of talk, that the good Antonio, the
honest Antonio,--O that I had a title good enough
to keep his name company!—

| | I wish the rumors were not true, in the way that a bitter widow tried to make her neighbors believe she cried for the death of her third husband. But it is true, without any wordiness or going on about the matter—the good Antonio, the honest Antonio—Oh, I just wish I had a title worthy enough to say how he is!— |

SALARINO
Come, the full stop.

| | C'mon, what's the story? |

SALANIO
Ha! what sayest thou? Why, the end is, he hath
lost a ship.

| | What are you saying? The point is, he has lost a ship. |

SALARINO
I would it might prove the end of his losses.

| | I would hope that is all he loses. |

SALANIO
Let me say 'amen' betimes, lest the devil cross my

prayer, for here he comes in the likeness of a Jew.

| | Let me say 'amen' at once unless the devil should cross the path of my prayer, for here comes the devil looking like a Jew. |

Enter SHYLOCK
How now, Shylock!
what news among the merchants?

SHYLOCK
You know, none so well, none so well as you,
of my daughter's flight.

SALARINO
That's certain: I, for my part, knew the tailor
that made the wings she flew withal.

SALANIO
And Shylock, for his own part, knew the bird was
fledged; and then it is the complexion of them all
to leave the dam.

SHYLOCK
She is damned for it.

SALANIO
That's certain, if the devil may be her judge.

SHYLOCK
My own flesh and blood to rebel!

SALANIO
Out upon it, old carrion! rebels it at these years?

SHYLOCK
I say, my daughter is my flesh and blood.

SALARINO
There is more difference between thy flesh
and hers
than between jet and ivory; more between your
bloods
than there is between red wine and rhenish. But
tell us, do you hear whether Antonio have had any
loss at sea or no?

SHYLOCK
There I have another bad match: a bankrupt, a
prodigal, who dare scarce show his head on the

Hey there, Shylock!
What's the news among the merchants?

You knew—nobody knew as well as you—
about my daughter's plans to flee.

That's true. I, myself, knew the tailor
who made the wings she flew away on.

And Shylock, for his part, knew she was ready
to run away—she had that look about her of
any child that is about to leave the home.

She is damned for it.

That would be for certain, if it's the devil
judging her.

My own flesh and blood turned against me!

Really? Your flesh turns against you at its
age?

I mean my daughter is my flesh and blood.

There is more difference between your flesh
and hers
than between black and white. And more
difference between your blood
than there is between red wine and white
wine. But tell us—have you heard whether
Antonio has had any loss at sea or not?

That's another bad bargain—a bankrupt, a
squanderer, who can hardly show his head on

Rialto; a beggar, that was used to come so smug upon	the Rialoto. A beggar who used to look so smug at
the mart; let him look to his bond: he was wont to	the market. Let him think about his loan. He was so ready to
call me usurer; let him look to his bond: he was	call me on my excessive interest. Let him think about his loan. He was
wont to lend money for a Christian courtesy; let him look to his bond.	willing to lend money interest free, but now let him think about his own loan.

SALARINO

Why, I am sure, if he forfeit, thou wilt not take his flesh: what's that good for?	Well, to be sure, if he forfeits it you won't take his flesh—what good would it be?

SHYLOCK

To bait fish withal: if it will feed nothing else,	I'll use it to bait fish. If it will feed nothing else
it will feed my revenge. He hath disgraced me, and hindered me half a million; laughed at my losses,	it will feed my revenge. He disgraces me and cost me a half million. He laughed at my losses,
mocked at my gains, scorned my nation, thwarted my bargains, cooled my friends, heated mine	mocked my gains, scorned my nation, defeated my bargins, caused my friends to turn against me, angered my
enemies; and what's his reason? I am a Jew. Hath	enemies, and for what? I am a Jew. That's why. Doesn't
not a Jew eyes? hath not a Jew hands, organs,	a Jew have eyes? Doesn't a Jew have hands, organs,
dimensions, senses, affections, passions? fed with	size, senses, feelings and emotions? We eat the
the same food, hurt with the same weapons, subject	same food, are wounded by the same weapons, susceptible
to the same diseases, healed by the same means,	to the same diseases, healed by the same methods,
warmed and cooled by the same winter and summer, as	warmed and cooled by the same winter and summer, just
a Christian is? If you prick us, do we not bleed?	like a Christian is? If you prick us, don't we bleed?
if you tickle us, do we not laugh? if you poison us, do we not die? and if you wrong us, shall we not	If you tickle us, don't we laugh? If you poison us, don't we die? And if you wrong us, won't we seek
revenge? If we are like you in the rest, we will	revenge? If we are like you in every other way, we will
resemble you in that. If a Jew wrong a Christian,	be like you in that way, too. If a Jew wronged a Christian

what is his humility? Revenge. If a Christian wrong a Jew, what should his sufferance be by Christian example? Why, revenge. The villany you teach me, I will execute, and it shall go hard but I will better the instruction.	what is his punishment? Revenge. If a Christian wrongs a Jew, what should his suffering be by the example of the Christian? Yes, revenge. The discourtesy you teach me, I will carry out, and I will do it more extremely than the way I learned it.

Enter a Servant

Servant Gentlemen, my master Antonio is at his house and desires to speak with you both.	Sirs, my master Antonio is at his house and he would like to speak to both of you.
SALARINO We have been up and down to seek him.	We've been looking all over for him.

Enter TUBAL

SALANIO Here comes another of the tribe: a third cannot be matched, unless the devil himself turn Jew.	Here comes another Jew—a third could do match these first two, unless the devil himself turned Jewish.

Exeunt SALANIO, SALARINO, and Servant

SHYLOCK How now, Tubal! what news from Genoa? hast thou found my daughter?	Hello, Tubal! What's the news from Genoa? Have you found my daughter?
TUBAL I often came where I did hear of her, but cannot find her.	I've heard talk about her in all the places I've been, but I haven't found her.
SHYLOCK Why, there, there, there, there! a diamond gone, cost me two thousand ducats in Frankfort! The curse never fell upon our nation till now; I never felt it till now: two thousand ducats in that; and other precious, precious jewels. I would my daughter were dead at my foot, and the jewels in her ear!	What, this is too much! A diamond gone that cost me two thousand ducats in Frankfort! The curse of being of Jew is something I have never felt until now. Two thousand ducats lost in that diamond, and other precious, precious jewels. I wish my daughter were dead at my feet with the jewels in her ears!

would she were hearsed at my foot, and the ducats in her coffin! No news of them? Why, so: and I know not what's spent in the search: why, thou loss upon loss! the thief gone with so much, and so much to find the thief; and no satisfaction, no revenge: nor no in luck stirring but what lights on my shoulders; no sighs but of my breathing; no tears but of my shedding.	I wish she were in a coffin at my feet, and the ducats were in the coffin with her! No news of them? I do not even know what I'm spending trying to find them. Loss after loss! The thief got away with so much, and it's taking so much to find the thief. And there's no satisfaction, no revenge. I've had no luck except the bad luck I'm having right now. No one is complaining about it but me. No one is crying except for my own tears.
TUBAL Yes, other men have ill luck too: Antonio, as I heard in Genoa,--	Well, other men are having bad luck, too. Antonio, as I heard in Genoa—
SHYLOCK What, what, what? ill luck, ill luck?	What? What? Bad luck? Bad luck?
TUBAL Hath an argosy cast away, coming from Tripolis.	His ship coming from Tripolis wrecked.
SHYLOCK I thank God, I thank God. Is't true, is't true?	Oh, thank God! Thank God! Is it true? Is it true?
TUBAL I spoke with some of the sailors that escaped The wreck.	I spoke with some of the sailors that survived the wreck.
SHYLOCK I thank thee, good Tubal: good news, good news! ha, ha! where? in Genoa?	Thank you, Tubal! That's good news! Good news! Ha ha! Where did you hear that? In Genoa?
TUBAL Your daughter spent in Genoa, as I heard, in one night fourscore ducats.	Your daughter spent a lot of money in Genoa. I heard in one night she spent eighty ducats.
SHYLOCK Thou stickest a dagger in me: I shall never see my gold again: fourscore ducats at a sitting! fourscore ducats!	Oh, you stick a knife in me! I will never see my gold again—eighty ducats in one night! Eighty ducats!

TUBAL
There came divers of Antonio's creditors in my company to Venice, that swear he cannot choose but break.

Several of Antonio's creditors who I traveled with to Venice swear that he has no choice but to break his promise to pay you.

SHYLOCK
I am very glad of it: I'll plague him; I'll torture him: I am glad of it.

I am glad to know this. I will torment and Torture him about it. I am glad to know this.

TUBAL
One of them showed me a ring that he had of your daughter for a monkey.

One of the creditors showed me a ring he had of yours that your daughter had given him to pay for a monkey.

SHYLOCK
Out upon her! Thou torturest me, Tubal: it was my

turquoise; I had it of Leah when I was a bachelor:

I would not have given it for a wilderness of monkeys.

I am so angry with her! That tortured me, Tubal—that was my turquoise ring. Leah gave it to me before we were married.
I would not have given it up for a jungle full of monkeys.

TUBAL
But Antonio is certainly undone.

Antonio is certainly ruined.

SHYLOCK
Nay, that's true, that's very true. Go, Tubal, fee me an officer; bespeak him a fortnight before. I

will have the heart of him, if he forfeit; for, were he out of Venice, I can make what merchandise I will. Go, go, Tubal, and meet me at our synagogue; go, good Tubal; at our synagogue, Tubal.

That's true, very true. Go, Tubal, and pay a police officer to arrest Antonio. Speak with him two weeks ahead of time. I will have the heart of Antonio if he forfeits. If he was not in Venice, I can make whatever deals I want. Go, go, Tubal, and meet me at our synagogue. Go, good Tubal. I'll see you there, Tubal.

Exeunt

SCENE II. Belmont. A room in PORTIA'S house.

Enter BASSANIO, PORTIA, GRATIANO, NERISSA, and Attendants

PORTIA I pray you, tarry: pause a day or two Before you hazard; for, in choosing wrong,	I beg you, please wait a day or two Before you make your guess. If you choose wrong
I lose your company: therefore forbear awhile. There's something tells me, but it is not love, I would not lose you; and you know yourself,	I will lose your company. So, wait awhile. There's something tells me, but it's not love, That I will not lose you, and you know yourself
Hate counsels not in such a quality. But lest you should not understand me well,--	That I would not feel that way if I hated you. But just in case you don't understand me well—
And yet a maiden hath no tongue but thought,--	And because girls aren't really supposed to say what's on our minds—
I would detain you here some month or two	I would like for you to stay here a month or two
Before you venture for me. I could teach you	Before you take a chance to win me. I could tell you
How to choose right, but I am then forsworn;	How to choose correctly, but I am sworn not to,
So will I never be: so may you miss me; But if you do, you'll make me wish a sin,	So I won't do that. So, you might lose me. But if you do, you'll make me wish I'd done the wrong thing—
That I had been forsworn. Beshrew your eyes,	That I had told you even though I swore I will not. Your eyes tempt me.
They have o'erlook'd me and divided me;	They have looked me over and have divided me.
One half of me is yours, the other half yours,	One half of me is yours, and the other half is yours, too—
Mine own, I would say; but if mine, then yours,	The half that should be mine, but if it's mine, then it's yours,
And so all yours. O, these naughty times Put bars between the owners and their rights!	So it is all yours. But these awful times Put obstacles between the owners and their claim!
And so, though yours, not yours. Prove it so,	And so, even so I am yours, I am not yours. If this proves to be the case
Let fortune go to hell for it, not I.	Then it is because luck has gone bad, not because of me.
I speak too long; but 'tis to peize the time, To eke it and to draw it out in length, To stay you from election.	I'm talking too much. It's just to prolong time, To stretch it out and draw it out, And to keep you from making your choice.

Original	Modern
BASSANIO Let me choose For as I am, I live upon the rack.	Let me choose. Not knowing like this is torturing me.
PORTIA Upon the rack, Bassanio! then confess What treason there is mingled with your love.	Punished for your crime, Bassanio! Then do confess What betrayal in mixed in with your love.
BASSANIO None but that ugly treason of mistrust, Which makes me fear the enjoying of my love: There may as well be amity and life 'Tween snow and fire, as treason and my love.	Simply the ugly betrayal of not being able to trust I will even be able to enjoy you as my love. There is as much relation between Snow and fire as there is between betrayal and my love for you.
PORTIA Ay, but I fear you speak upon the rack, Where men enforced do speak anything.	Ah, but I'm afraid you might be speaking like one who is being punished Who will say anything under the stress.
BASSANIO Promise me life, and I'll confess the truth.	Promise you will let me live and I'll confess the truth.
PORTIA Well then, confess and live.	Well, in that case, confess and live.
BASSANIO 'Confess' and 'love' Had been the very sum of my confession: O happy torment, when my torturer Doth teach me answers for deliverance! But let me to my fortune and the caskets.	'Confess' and 'love' Is what my confession amounts to: Oh, what happy torture, when my tormenter Tells me the answers that set me free! But please let me take my chances with the trunks.
PORTIA Away, then! I am lock'd in one of them: If you do love me, you will find me out. Nerissa and the rest, stand all aloof. Let music sound while he doth make his choice; Then, if he lose, he makes a swan-like end, Fading in music: that the comparison	Well, let's go then! I am locked inside one of them. If you love me, you will figure out which one. Nerissa and everybody else, stand back from him. Let music play while he makes his choice. Then, if he loses, he will find his swan-song In the music. To make it even more so

May stand more proper, my eye shall be the stream	*And proper like a swan-song, my eyes will cry the tears to make a stream*
And watery death-bed for him. He may win;	*Which will be the watery death bed of the swan. But he might win.*
And what is music then? Then music is	*What music should we play in that case? That music*
Even as the flourish when true subjects bow	*Should be like the fanfare that loyal subjects bow*
To a new-crowned monarch: such it is	*To when a king is newly crowned. Just like*
As are those dulcet sounds in break of day	*The sweet music that plays at daybreak*
That creep into the dreaming bridegroom's ear,	*That a drowsy bridegroom hears*
And summon him to marriage. Now he goes,	*When he wakes on his wedding day. Bassanio is walking toward the trunks*
With no less presence, but with much more love,	*with no less dignity but with much more love*
Than young Alcides, when he did redeem	*Than the young Hercules when he freed*
The virgin tribute paid by howling Troy	*The virgin princess sacrificed at Troy*
To the sea-monster: I stand for sacrifice	*From the sea monster. I'll be like the princess*
The rest aloof are the Dardanian wives,	*And everyone else can be like wives at Troy*
With bleared visages, come forth to view	*Crying as we look on and watch to see*
The issue of the exploit. Go, Hercules!	*The result of the challenge. Go, Hercules!*
Live thou, I live: with much, much more dismay	*If you live, I live. I feel much, much more distress*
I view the fight than thou that makest the fray.	*Watching the struggle than you feel in making it.*

Music, whilst BASSANIO comments on the caskets to himself

SONG.
Tell me where is fancy bred,	*Tell me where is love born,*
Or in the heart, or in the head?	*In the heart or in the head?*
How begot, how nourished?	*How is it started and how is it fed?*
Reply, reply.	*Answer. Answer.*
It is engender'd in the eyes,	*It starts in the eyes,*
With gazing fed; and fancy dies	*And is fed with gazes, and love dies*
In the cradle where it lies.	*When it is still just an infant.*
Let us all ring fancy's knell	*Let us all ring bells to mourn love's passing*
I'll begin it,--Ding, dong, bell.	*I'll start—Ding, dong, bell.*

ALL
Ding, dong, bell.	*Ding, dong, bell.*

BASSANIO
So may the outward shows be least themselves:	*What shows on the outside does not reveal what is inside:*
The world is still deceived with ornament.	*The world is often deceived with pretty attire.*

Original	Modern
In law, what plea so tainted and corrupt,	In the court, people can plead not guilty when they are tainted and corrupt,
But, being seasoned with a gracious voice,	And if they do in a pleasing voice
Obscures the show of evil? In religion,	May cover any signs of guilt. In religion,
What damned error, but some sober brow	Some men can defend a sinful act by putting on a serious face
Will bless it and approve it with a text,	And make it seem good by reading from the Bible,
Hiding the grossness with fair ornament?	And in that way hide the sin with pretty words.
There is no vice so simple but assumes	There is no common sin that can't be made to take on
Some mark of virtue on his outward parts:	The appearance of seeming good by changing how it looks.
How many cowards, whose hearts are all as false	How many cowards, whose courage is about as strong
As stairs of sand, wear yet upon their chins	As a staircase made of sand, wear on their chins
The beards of Hercules and frowning Mars;	Beards like Hercules or Mars, the god of war,
Who, inward search'd, have livers white as milk;	Even though if you look inside you will find them fearful?
And these assume but valour's excrement	But they wear these beards as signs of strength
To render them redoubted! Look on beauty,	To try to make people afraid of them! Look at beauty, too—
And you shall see 'tis purchased by the weight;	And you will see it can be acquired with lots of makeup,
Which therein works a miracle in nature,	Which works miracles on natural looks,
Making them lightest that wear most of it:	Making those that wear it most seem promiscious.
So are those crisped snaky golden locks	It's the same thing with curly, blond hair—
Which make such wanton gambols with the wind,	Which blows so playfully and spirited in the wind,
Upon supposed fairness, often known	And is supposed to make a woman seem more beautiful, but it is
To be the dowry of a second head,	Often a wig made from the head of a woman
The skull that bred them in the sepulchre.	Whose skull is in the grave.
Thus ornament is but the guiled shore	So outward beauty is but a golden shore
To a most dangerous sea; the beauteous scarf	Leading to a dangerous sea, like a beautiful scarf
Veiling an Indian beauty; in a word,	Can hide a dark woman. Plainly put—
The seeming truth which cunning times put on	What seems to be true is often a cunning disguise
To entrap the wisest. Therefore, thou gaudy gold,	To trap even the wisest. So because of this, you brilliant gold—

Original	Modern
Hard food for Midas, I will none of thee;	Unpleasant food for Midas to eat—I won't choose.
Nor none of thee, thou pale and common drudge	And not the pale silver, either, which serves as a slave
'Tween man and man: but thou, thou meagre lead,	As coins for men to do business. But you, lead, that is of no real value
Which rather threatenest than dost promise aught,	And which looks more threatening than promising,
Thy paleness moves me more than eloquence; And here choose I; joy be the consequence!	And which moves me beyond eloquence— It is the one I choose. I hope I'm happy with the outcome.

PORTIA
[Aside]
Original	Modern
How all the other passions fleet to air, As doubtful thoughts, and rash-embraced despair,	[Aside] All my other feelings are flying to the air— Doubtful thoughts and quickly embraced sadness,
And shuddering fear, and green-eyed jealousy! O love, Be moderate; allay thy ecstasy,	And fear that left me shaking and awful O jealousy—they all leave! Oh, I feel love, And I need to take things slowly and quiet my happiness,
In measure rein thy joy; scant this excess.	I need to contain my joy and try not to feel so much.
I feel too much thy blessing: make it less,	I'm feeling too much happiness. I need to feel less
For fear I surfeit.	Because I am afraid I feel too much.

BASSANIO
Original	Modern
What find I here?	What's in here?

Opening the leaden casket
Original	Modern
Fair Portia's counterfeit! What demi-god Hath come so near creation? Move these eyes?	Beautiful Portia's picture! What God-like Artist made this picture that looks so much like her? Are the eyes moving?
Or whether, riding on the balls of mine, Seem they in motion? Here are sever'd lips, Parted with sugar breath: so sweet a bar Should sunder such sweet friends. Here in her hairs The painter plays the spider and hath woven A golden mesh to entrap the hearts of men,	Or do they just seem to be moving when I move my eyes? Look are her open lips Parted with sweet breath—so sweet a way To part such sweet lips. Here in her hair The painter played like a spider and wove A golden mesh that can entrap the hearts of men
Faster than gnats in cobwebs; but her eyes,--	Faster than small flies in cobwebs. But her eyes—
How could he see to do them? having made one,	How could he keep looking to paint them? After he painted the first,

Methinks it should have power to steal both his	It seems it would have the power to make him stop seeing
And leave itself unfurnish'd. Yet look, how far	And unable to paint the second one. But look, how much
The substance of my praise doth wrong this shadow	The subject of the picture I praise outdoes its shadow
In underprizing it, so far this shadow	And makes it seem small, and the picture is nowhere as beautiful
Doth limp behind the substance. Here's the scroll,	As its subject. Here's a paper
The continent and summary of my fortune.	That contains the summary of my fortune.
Reads	
You that choose not by the view,	You who has chosen not by looks
Chance as fair and choose as true!	Have had good luck and made the right choice!
Since this fortune falls to you,	Since this good fortune falls to you,
Be content and seek no new,	Be happy and seek nothing else.
If you be well pleased with this	If you are happy with this
And hold your fortune for your bliss,	And accept this fortune for your state of being,
Turn you where your lady is	Turn toward where your lady is
And claim her with a loving kiss.	And claim her as yours with a loving kiss.
A gentle scroll. Fair lady, by your leave;	A nice note. Fair lady, with your permission,
I come by note, to give and to receive.	This note tells me to give you a kiss and to receive you.
Like one of two contending in a prize,	But like someone struggling in a contest,
That thinks he hath done well in people's eyes,	That things he has done well in people's eyes,
Hearing applause and universal shout,	Draws applause and shouting—
Giddy in spirit, still gazing in a doubt	I am still excited and energized, but wondering and not sure
Whether these pearls of praise be his or no;	Whether this praise is mine or not.
So, thrice fair lady, stand I, even so;	So, wonderfully beautiful lady, I'm standing here,
As doubtful whether what I see be true,	Doubting if what I see is true,
Until confirm'd, sign'd, ratified by you.	Until it is confirmed, signed and made official by you.
PORTIA	
You see me, Lord Bassanio, where I stand,	You see me, Lord Bassanio, as I stand here,
Such as I am: though for myself alone	And I am what I am, though I alone wouldn't wish
I would not be ambitious in my wish,	To be better for myself,
To wish myself much better; yet, for you	I wish I could be better for you.
I would be trebled twenty times myself;	I would be twenty times what I am—
A thousand times more fair, ten thousand times more rich;	A thousand times more beautiful and ten thousand times richer—
That only to stand high in your account,	So you might value me more.

I might in virtue, beauties, livings, friends, Exceed account; but the full sum of me	My talents, beauties, possessions and friends, Would be more than you could want. However, the full worth of me
Is sum of something, which, to term in gross, Is an unlesson'd girl, unschool'd, unpractised;	Is something that amounts to the total of An unlearned girl—uneducated and innocent—
Happy in this, she is not yet so old But she may learn; happier than this,	And happy that she is not too old That she can learn new things, and even happier
She is not bred so dull but she can learn;	That she was not raised without the ability to be capable of learning,
Happiest of all is that her gentle spirit Commits itself to yours to be directed, As from her lord, her governor, her king. Myself and what is mine to you and yours Is now converted: but now I was the lord Of this fair mansion, master of my servants,	And happiest of all that her spirit Commits itself to you to be taught. By her lord, her governor, her king. Myself and all that is mine is now to you Transferred. Until now I was the lord Of this beautiful mansion. I was master of my servants,
Queen o'er myself: and even now, but now, This house, these servants and this same myself Are yours, my lord: I give them with this ring;	And Queen of myself. But even as we speak This house, these servants and even me Are yours, my lord. I give them to you with this ring.
Which when you part from, lose, or give away, Let it presage the ruin of your love And be my vantage to exclaim on you.	If you ever part with it, lose it or give it away, It means our love is over, And I'll have the right to be angry with you.
BASSANIO Madam, you have bereft me of all words, Only my blood speaks to you in my veins;	Madam, you've left me speechless. My blood is pounding in my veins in response to you.
And there is such confusion in my powers, As after some oration fairly spoke By a beloved prince, there doth appear Among the buzzing pleased multitude; Where every something, being blent together, Turns to a wild of nothing, save of joy, Express'd and not express'd. But when this ring	I feel so confused right now about everything, Like after there is a wonderful speech Made by a prince you admire, and among The crowd is applause and cheers. Everything—all blending together— Becomes nothing but wild joy Both shouted and not shouted about. If this ring
Parts from this finger, then parts life from hence:	Ever leaves my finger, you can be sure I am dead.
O, then be bold to say Bassanio's dead!	You can declare with certainty, 'Bassanio's dead!'
NERISSA My lord and lady, it is now our time,	My lord and my lady, it is now time

That have stood by and seen our wishes prosper, | For us who have been watching this to make our wishes known
To cry, good joy: good joy, my lord and lady! | And to say, Best wishes! Best wishes, my lord and lady!

GRATIANO
My lord Bassanio and my gentle lady, | My lord Bassanio and my gentle lady,
I wish you all the joy that you can wish; | I wish you all the happiness you could possible want,

For I am sure you can wish none from me: | And I am sure I can wish you no more.
And when your honours mean to solemnize | When you are ready to take your vows
The bargain of your faith, I do beseech you, | To become married, I want to ask
Even at that time I may be married too. | If I may get married at the same time as you.

BASSANIO
With all my heart, so thou canst get a wife. | Certainly, if you can find a wife by then.

GRATIANO
I thank your lordship, you have got me one. | Thank you, my lord, I have gotten one because of you.

My eyes, my lord, can look as swift as yours: | I fall in love as quickly as you do—at first sight.

You saw the mistress, I beheld the maid; | Just as when you fell when you saw Portia, I looked at Nerrisa

You loved, I loved for intermission. | And fell in love as quickly as you.
No more pertains to me, my lord, than you. | We both have the same right to do so.
Your fortune stood upon the casket there, | Just as your fortune depended on the trunks,
And so did mine too, as the matter falls; | So did mine, and I got right to the matter
For wooing here until I sweat again, | Of wooing her until I began to sweat
And sweating until my very roof was dry | And making more effort until my mouth was dry,

With oaths of love, at last, if promise last, | From declarations of love and promises
I got a promise of this fair one here | Until I got a promise from this beautiful lady
To have her love, provided that your fortune | That we would marry dependent on fortune
Achieved her mistress. | Of winning her mistress.

PORTIA
Is this true, Nerissa? | Is this true, Nerissa?

NERISSA
Madam, it is, so you stand pleased withal. | Yes, Madam, if you say it is okay.

BASSANIO
And do you, Gratiano, mean good faith? | And do you mean what you say, Gratiano?

GRATIANO
Yes, faith, my lord.

Yes, I mean it, my lord.

BASSANIO
Our feast shall be much honour'd in your marriage.

We would be honored to include you in our marriage feast.

GRATIANO
We'll play with them the first boy for a thousand ducats.

Let's bet them a thousand ducats that we'll have the first son.

NERISSA
What, and stake down?

What, and put it down now?

GRATIANO
No; we shall ne'er win at that sport, and stake down.
But who comes here? Lorenzo and his infidel?
What, and my old Venetian friend Salerio?

*No, we'd never win the bet if I put it down!
Who's coming? Lorenzo and his pagan?
Look, is it really my old Venetian friend Salerio?*

Enter LORENZO, JESSICA, and SALERIO, a Messenger from Venice

BASSANIO
Lorenzo and Salerio, welcome hither;
If that the youth of my new interest here
Have power to bid you welcome. By your leave,

I bid my very friends and countrymen,
Sweet Portia, welcome.

*Lorenzo and Salerio, welcome!
I hope my new position as master of the house
Has enough power to bid you welcome. If it's alright with you,
I give my friends and countrymen
a welcome, sweet Portia.*

PORTIA
So do I, my lord:
They are entirely welcome.

*So do I, my lord.
They are totally welcome.*

LORENZO
I thank your honour. For my part, my lord,
My purpose was not to have seen you here;
But meeting with Salerio by the way,
He did entreat me, past all saying nay,
To come with him along.

*Thank you. It wasn't my intention, my lord,
To come here to see you.
I met with Salerio along the way
And he insisted, with no room for me to say no, That I come along with him!*

SALERIO
I did, my lord;
And I have reason for it. Signior Antonio
Commends him to you.

*I did that, my lord,
And I have good reason. Signior Antonio
Sends his grettings.*

Gives Bassanio a letter

BASSANIO
Ere I ope his letter,
I pray you, tell me how my good friend doth.

Before I open this,
Please tell me how Antonio is doing.

SALERIO
Not sick, my lord, unless it be in mind;
Nor well, unless in mind: his letter there

He's not sick, my lord, but he is worried.
He's not well, but he is very worried. This letter

Will show you his estate.

Will reveal what's going on.

GRATIANO
Nerissa, cheer yon stranger; bid her welcome.

Nerrisa, welcome this man. Say hello to her, too,

Your hand, Salerio: what's the news from Venice?
How doth that royal merchant, good Antonio?
I know he will be glad of our success;
We are the Jasons, we have won the fleece.

Salerio. What's the word from Venice?
How is the merchant Antonio doing?
I know he will be glad to hear of our success.
We are the Jasons who have won the Golden Fleece.

SALERIO
I would you had won the fleece that he hath lost.

I wish you had won what he has lost.

PORTIA
There are some shrewd contents in yon same paper,

Whatever is written in that letter is hard news—

That steals the colour from Bassanio's cheek:
Some dear friend dead; else nothing in the world

It is making Bassanio turn pale to read it.
Some dear friend must have died—I can't think of anything else in the world

Could turn so much the constitution
Of any constant man. What, worse and worse!

That would change the mood
Of a stable man so much. Look! He seems worse and worse!

With leave, Bassanio: I am half yourself,

With your permission, Bassanio: I am your other half,

And I must freely have the half of anything
That this same paper brings you.

So let me bear half of whatever it is
This letter brings to you.

BASSANIO
O sweet Portia,
Here are a few of the unpleasant'st words
That ever blotted paper! Gentle lady,
When I did first impart my love to you,
I freely told you, all the wealth I had

Oh sweet Portia,
What is here are the most unpleasant words
That ever stained paper! Kind lady,
When I first told you I love you,
I told you that all the wealth I have

Original	Modern
Ran in my veins, I was a gentleman;	Runs in my veins—that I was born noble,
And then I told you true: and yet, dear lady,	And then I told you the truth, but still, dear lady,
Rating myself at nothing, you shall see	When I said I have nothing, you will see
How much I was a braggart. When I told you	That I was bragging. When I said
My state was nothing, I should then have told you	I had nothing, I should have told you, as well,
That I was worse than nothing; for, indeed,	That I have worse than nothing, for, it's true,
I have engaged myself to a dear friend,	I asked a favor of a dear frined,
Engaged my friend to his mere enemy,	And he borrowed money from his enemy
To feed my means. Here is a letter, lady;	To help me out. In this letter, lady,
The paper as the body of my friend,	The paper seems like the body of my friend.
And every word in it a gaping wound,	With every word like a huge wound
Issuing life-blood. But is it true, Salerio?	bleeding all over the place. Is it true, Salerio,
Have all his ventures fail'd? What, not one hit?	Have all his ships at sea failed? Did not one survive?
From Tripolis, from Mexico and England,	From Tripolos and Mexico and England,
From Lisbon, Barbary and India?	From Lisbon, Barbary and India?
And not one vessel 'scape the dreadful touch	Not one of the ships escaped being wrecked
Of merchant-marring rocks?	On merchant-ruining rocks?
SALERIO	
Not one, my lord.	Not one, my lord.
Besides, it should appear, that if he had	Besides, it looks as though even if he had
The present money to discharge the Jew,	The money to pay off the Jew,
He would not take it. Never did I know	The Jew would not take it. Never have I known
A creature, that did bear the shape of man,	A creature that looked so much like a man
So keen and greedy to confound a man:	So ready and eager to ruin a man.
He plies the duke at morning and at night,	He's at the duke both morning and night
And doth impeach the freedom of the state,	Saying the freedom of the state will be harmed
If they deny him justice: twenty merchants,	If they deny him justice. Twenty merchants,
The duke himself, and the magnificoes	The duke himself, and the Venetian leaders
Of greatest port, have all persuaded with him;	Of highest standing have all tried to convince him,
But none can drive him from the envious plea	But no one can convince his not to go after the claim
Of forfeiture, of justice and his bond.	Written in the loan papers regarding non-payment.
JESSICA	
When I was with him I have heard him swear	When I was with my father I heard him swear
To Tubal and to Chus, his countrymen,	To Tubal and to Chus, fellow Jews,
That he would rather have Antonio's flesh	That he would rather have Antonio's flesh
Than twenty times the value of the sum	Than twenty times the value of the loaned amount
That he did owe him: and I know, my lord,	That Antonio owed him. And I know, my lord,

If law, authority and power deny not,	That is the law, authory and power can not stop it,
It will go hard with poor Antonio.	It will be hard for poor Antonio.

PORTIA
Is it your dear friend that is thus in trouble?	Is it your dear friend who is in this trouble?

BASSANIO
The dearest friend to me, the kindest man,	He is my dearest friend and the kindest man.
The best-condition'd and unwearied spirit	He had the best disposition and a great spirit
In doing courtesies, and one in whom	And has the best manners. He is the sort of man
The ancient Roman honour more appears	The ancient Roman idea of honor appears in
Than any that draws breath in Italy.	More than any other man in Italy.

PORTIA
What sum owes he the Jew?	How much does he owe the Jew?

BASSANIO
For me three thousand ducats.	He owes him three thousand ducats.

PORTIA
What, no more?	What, that's all?
Pay him six thousand, and deface the bond;	Pay him six thousand and be done with the debt.
Double six thousand, and then treble that,	Double the six thousand, and then triple it
Before a friend of this description	Before this great friend as you've described him
Shall lose a hair through Bassanio's fault.	Loses a hair through your fault.
First go with me to church and call me wife,	But first, let's go to church and get married.
And then away to Venice to your friend;	And then you should go to Venice to be with your friend.
For never shall you lie by Portia's side	You would never sleep by my side otherwise
With an unquiet soul. You shall have gold	Without a restless soul. You will have enough
To pay the petty debt twenty times over:	gold to pay this petty debt twenty times over.
When it is paid, bring your true friend along.	When it is paid, bring your friend back here.
My maid Nerissa and myself meantime	Nerissa and I, in the meantime
Will live as maids and widows. Come, away!	Will live like virgins and widows. Let's go!
For you shall hence upon your wedding-day:	You will leave once you are married.
Bid your friends welcome, show a merry cheer:	Welcome your friends and put on a happy face.
Since you are dear bought, I will love you dear.	Since it is costing so much to have you, I will love you all the more.
But let me hear the letter of your friend.	But first, read me the letter from your friend.

BASSANIO
[Reads]
Sweet Bassanio, my ships have all
miscarried, my creditors grow cruel, my estate is

very low, my bond to the Jew is forfeit; and since

in paying it, it is impossible I should live, all
debts are cleared between you and I, if I might but

see you at my death. Notwithstanding, use your
pleasure: if your love do not persuade you to come,
let not my letter.

PORTIA
O love, dispatch all business, and be gone!

BASSANIO
Since I have your good leave to go away,
I will make haste: but, till I come again,
No bed shall e'er be guilty of my stay,
No rest be interposer 'twixt us twain.

Exeunt

[Reads]
Sweer Bassanio, my ships have all been wrecked, my creditors are growing cruel, my wealth is very low, my loan to the Jew is forfeited, and since I'm not paying it, it is impossible to live, all debts between you and I are cleared if I could just see you when I die. I understand that if you don't want to come because of your affection for me this letter will not convince you to do so.

Oh, my love—take care of things and go on!

Since I have your blessing in going away,
I will hurry back. But, until I return,
Know that I will not sleep in any bed.
I will not rest until I am with you again.

SCENE III. Venice. A street.

Enter SHYLOCK, SALARINO, ANTONIO, and Gaoler

SHYLOCK
Gaoler, look to him: tell not me of mercy;

This is the fool that lent out money gratis:

Gaoler, look to him.

ANTONIO
Hear me yet, good Shylock.

SHYLOCK
I'll have my bond; speak not against my bond:

I have sworn an oath that I will have my bond.

Thou call'dst me dog before thou hadst a cause;

But, since I am a dog, beware my fangs:
The duke shall grant me justice. I do wonder,
Thou naughty gaoler, that thou art so fond
To come abroad with him at his request.

ANTONIO
I pray thee, hear me speak.

SHYLOCK
I'll have my bond; I will not hear thee speak:

I'll have my bond; and therefore speak no more.
I'll not be made a soft and dull-eyed fool,

To shake the head, relent, and sigh, and yield

To Christian intercessors. Follow not;
I'll have no speaking: I will have my bond.

Exit

SALARINO

Jailer, keep an eye on this one. Don't try to convince me of mercy.
This is the fool that lent out money without interest.
Jailer, keep an eye on him.

Listen to me, Shylock.

I'll have my payment. Don't try to talk me out of getting it.
I have sworn an oath the I will get my payment.
You called me a dog when you had no reason to do so.
So, since I am a dog, beware of my fangs. The duke will give me justice. I do wonder, however, why this jailer is so bad, to allow Antonio to come out of his cell by simply asking.

Please, listen to what I have to say.

I will have my payment. I will not listen to you.
I will have my payment. So just stop talking. I'll not be made to look like a weak and easily deceived fool
To just shake my head, give up to you with a sigh and yield
To Christian prayers. Don't follow me.
I won't listen to you. I will have my payment.

It is the most impenetrable cur That ever kept with men.	He is the most impossible dog Who ever lived among men.
ANTONIO Let him alone: I'll follow him no more with bootless prayers.	Leave him alone. I won't follow him anymore with my useless prayers.
He seeks my life; his reason well I know: I oft deliver'd from his forfeitures	He wants me dead. I know his reason: I've given money to the people who couldn't pay him back
Many that have at times made moan to me; Therefore he hates me.	Many times, once they've asked me to do so. He hates me for that reason.
SALARINO I am sure the duke Will never grant this forfeiture to hold.	I am sure the duke Will never allow this payment for forfeit to be enforced.
ANTONIO The duke cannot deny the course of law: For the commodity that strangers have With us in Venice, if it be denied, Will much impeach the justice of his state;	The duke cannot deny the law. The business that strangers bring To merchants in Venice can not be denied Or it would cause harm to the justice of the state
Since that the trade and profit of the city	Since the profit of the city depends on the trade
Consisteth of all nations. Therefore, go: These griefs and losses have so bated me,	Of foreigners. So, go on— These worries have caused me to lose so much weight
That I shall hardly spare a pound of flesh To-morrow to my bloody creditor. Well, gaoler, on. Pray God, Bassanio come	I will hardly be able to spare a pound of flesh Tomorrow to my bloody creditor. So, jailer, go away. I just hope to God Bassanio comes
To see me pay his debt, and then I care not!	To see me pay his debt, and I don't care about anything else!

Exeunt

SCENE IV. Belmont. A room in PORTIA'S house.

Enter PORTIA, NERISSA, LORENZO, JESSICA, and BALTHASAR

LORENZO
Madam, although I speak it in your presence,
You have a noble and a true conceit
Of godlike amity; which appears most strongly
In bearing thus the absence of your lord.
But if you knew to whom you show this honour,
How true a gentleman you send relief,
How dear a lover of my lord your husband,
I know you would be prouder of the work
Than customary bounty can enforce you.

PORTIA
I never did repent for doing good,
Nor shall not now: for in companions
That do converse and waste the time together,
Whose souls do bear an equal yoke Of love,
There must be needs a like proportion
Of lineaments, of manners and of spirit;
Which makes me think that this Antonio,
Being the bosom lover of my lord,
Must needs be like my lord. If it be so,
How little is the cost I have bestow'd
In purchasing the semblance of my soul
From out the state of hellish misery!
This comes too near the praising of myself;
Therefore no more of it: hear other things.
Lorenzo, I commit into your hands
The husbandry and manage of my house
Until my lord's return: for mine own part,
I have toward heaven breathed a secret vow
To live in prayer and contemplation,
Only attended by Nerissa here,
Until her husband and my lord's return:
There is a monastery two miles off;
And there will we abide. I do desire you
Not to deny this imposition;
The which my love and some necessity
Now lays upon you.

LORENZO

---

*Madam, I'd like to say in your presence
That you have a noble and true understanding
Of real friendship, which you have shown
By letting your lord go off like this.*

*The man you are sending him to
Loves your lord greatly and is faithful to him.
I know you might be prouder of doing what
comes natural to you if you knew this.*

*I've never been sorry for doing good,
And I won't be now. Friends
That talk and spend time together
Have souls that bear an equal amount of love.
They must be very much alike, and have the
same sort of chracteristics, manners and
energy. This makes me think that this Antonio,
Being such a close friend of my lord,
Must be very much like my lord. So, if that's
the case, The money I've sent with him is a
small amount To free the one who is like my
lover Out of a hellish state!
But, I'm coming too close to praising myself,
So let's talk of this no more. Let's talk about
other things. Lorenzo, I'd like for you
To take over the care and management of my
house Until my lord comes back. As for me—
I have made a secret vow to heaven
To live in prayer and meditation
To be only accompanied my Nerissa
Until her husband and my lord come back.
There is a monastery about two miles away.
We will stay there. I hope you
Will not deny this request
Which my love and some need
Puts upon you.*

Madam, with all my heart;
I shall obey you in all fair commands.

PORTIA
My people do already know my mind,
And will acknowledge you and Jessica
In place of Lord Bassanio and myself.
And so farewell, till we shall meet again.

LORENZO
Fair thoughts and happy hours attend on you!

JESSICA
I wish your ladyship all heart's content.

PORTIA
I thank you for your wish, and am well pleased
To wish it back on you: fare you well Jessica.

Exeunt JESSICA and LORENZO

Now, Balthasar,
As I have ever found thee honest-true,
So let me find thee still. Take this same letter,
And use thou all the endeavour of a man
In speed to Padua: see thou render this
Into my cousin's hand, Doctor Bellario;
And, look, what notes and garments he doth give thee,
Bring them, I pray thee, with imagined speed
Unto the tranect, to the common ferry
Which trades to Venice. Waste no time in words,
But get thee gone: I shall be there before thee.

BALTHASAR
Madam, I go with all convenient speed.

Exit

PORTIA
Come on, Nerissa; I have work in hand
That you yet know not of: we'll see our husbands
Before they think of us.

Madam, with all of my heart—
I will do whatever you wish.

My servants already know about this
And will answer to you and Jessica
In place of Lord Bassanio and me.
So, goodbye, until we see each other again.

I hope you find peace of mind and happiness!

I wish you all you hope for at this time.

Thanks you for the wish, and I'm happy
To wish the same back to you. Goodbye,
Jessica. Take care.

Now, Balthasar,
I have found you to be ever honest and true,
And I hope to find you that way, still. Take this
letter. And with as much speed as possible for
a man Get to Padua. Put this letter
Into my cousin's—Dr. Bellario—hands.
Take whatever papers and clothes he gives to you
And bring them, please, as quickly as you can
To the ferry—the public ferry—
That goes to and from Venice. Don't waste
time talking. Just get going. I will be there
before you.

Madam, I will go as fast as possible.

Come on, Nerissa, I have things in the works
You don't know about yet. We'll see our
husbands before they even think of us.

NERISSA
Shall they see us?

Will they see us?

PORTIA
They shall, Nerissa; but in such a habit,
That they shall think we are accomplished
With that we lack. I'll hold thee any wager,
When we are both accoutred like young men,
I'll prove the prettier fellow of the two,
And wear my dagger with the braver grace,
And speak between the change of man and boy
With a reed voice, and turn two mincing steps
Into a manly stride, and speak of frays
Like a fine bragging youth, and tell quaint lies,

How honourable ladies sought my love,
Which I denying, they fell sick and died;
I could not do withal; then I'll repent,
And wish for all that, that I had not killed them;
And twenty of these puny lies I'll tell,

That men shall swear I have discontinued school
Above a twelvemonth. I have within my mind
A thousand raw tricks of these bragging Jacks,
Which I will practise.

*They will see us, Nerissa, but we will be dressed In a way that they will think we are what we are not. I will bet you That when we are both dressed like young men I will be the handsomer of the two And I will wear my sword with much more grace and speak like just like an adolescent boy with a squeaking voice, and my ladylike steps will become a manly stride. I'll talk about frightening things like a fine bragging young man, and tell clever lies About how honorable ladies wanted my love, But when I wouldn't give it to them, they fell sick and died I could do nothing about it! Then, I'll feel sorry and wish that what I had done had not killed them. I'll tell twenty of these little lies.
And men will swear I just graduated from school a year ago. I have in my head A thousand of these sort of tricks for young men that I will use.*

NERISSA
Why, shall we turn to men?

Why will we turn into men?

PORTIA
Fie, what a question's that,
If thou wert near a lewd interpreter!
But come, I'll tell thee all my whole device
When I am in my coach, which stays for us
At the park gate; and therefore haste away,
For we must measure twenty miles to-day.

*What sort of question is that!
As if you were an improper interviewer!
But, come on, I'll tell you the whole plan When we are in my coach which is waiting for us at the park gate. We must hurry away.
We have to make at least twenty miles today.*

Exeunt

SCENE V. The same. A garden.

Enter LAUNCELOT and JESSICA

LAUNCELOT
Yes, truly; for, look you, the sins of the father are to be laid upon the children: therefore, I promise ye, I fear you. I was always plain with you, and so now I speak my agitation of the matter: therefore be of good cheer, for truly I think you are damned. There is but one hope in it that can do you any good; and that is but a kind of bastard hope neither.

	Yes, it's true. Look—the sins of fathers Are paid for by their children. So, I I worried for you. I've always been direct with you and so I will say what is bothering me in this case: Be happy, for I really think you are going to hell. There is only one hope for you, but that is a sort of illegitimate hope.

JESSICA
And what hope is that, I pray thee?

Tell me, what hope is that?

LAUNCELOT
Marry, you may partly hope that your father got you not, that you are not the Jew's daughter.

Well, you can hope that your father is not your father, and that you are not the Jew's daughter.

JESSICA
That were a kind of bastard hope, indeed: so the sins of my mother should be visited upon me.

That would be an illegitimate hope, yes, and the sins of my mother would be upon me in that case.

LAUNCELOT
Truly then I fear you are damned both by father And mother: thus when I shun Scylla, your father, I fall into Charybdis, your mother: well, you are gone both ways.

Well, in that case, I'm afraid you will go to hell because of your father and your mother. If you do not fall into one trap—your father—you will fall into the other one—your mother. So, you are a goner either way.

JESSICA
I shall be saved by my husband; he hath made me a Christian.

I will be saved by my husband. He has made me a Christian.

LAUNCELOT
Truly, the more to blame he: we were Christians enow before; e'en as many as could well live, one by another. This making Christians will raise the price of hogs: if we grow all to be pork-eaters, we shall not shortly have a rasher on the coals for money.

Well, he was wrong to do that. There were plenty of Christians before—as many as could stand to live near one another. Making more Christians will raise the price of pigs. We we all become pork-eaters, we will soon not even be able to afford a slice of bacon.

Enter LORENZO

JESSICA
I'll tell my husband, Launcelot, what you say:
here he comes.

LORENZO
I shall grow jealous of you shortly, Launcelot, if
you thus get my wife into corners.

JESSICA
Nay, you need not fear us, Lorenzo:
Launcelot and I are out.
are out. He tells me flatly, there is no mercy for
me in heaven, because I am a Jew's daughter:
and he says, you are no good member of the
commonwealth, for in converting Jews to
Christians, you raise the price of pork.

LORENZO
I shall answer that better to the commonwealth than
you can the getting up of the negro's belly: the
Moor is with child by you, Launcelot.
child, Launcelot.

LAUNCELOT
It is much that the Moor should be more than
reason:
but if she be less than an honest woman, she is
indeed more than I took her for.

LORENZO
How every fool can play upon the word! I think the
best grace of wit will shortly turn into silence,
and discourse grow commendable in none only but
parrots. Go in, sirrah; bid them prepare for dinner.

LAUNCELOT
That is done, sir; they have all stomachs.

LORENZO
Goodly Lord, what a wit-snapper are you! then bid
them prepare dinner.

LAUNCELOT

That is done too, sir; only 'cover' is the word.

I believe the term you are looking for, sir, it 'set the table.'

LORENZO
Will you cover then, sir?

Will you set the table then?

LAUNCELOT
Not so, sir, neither; I know my duty.

No sir, that is not my responsibility.

LORENZO
Yet more quarrelling with occasion!
Wilt thou show
the whole wealth of thy wit in an instant? I pray

tree, understand a plain man in his plain meaning:
go to thy fellows; bid them cover the table, serve
in the meat, and we will come in to dinner.

You're just finding reasons to be clever! Are you going to show me the entire range of you cleverness all at once? Please, Just understand very plainly what I mean: Go in there and tell the servants to set the table, serve the meet and we will come in and eat it.

LAUNCELOT
For the table, sir, it shall be served in; for the
meat, sir, it shall be covered; for your coming in
to dinner, sir, why, let it be as humours and
conceits shall govern.

Regarding the table, sir, the food will be served on it. Regarding the meat, sir, it will be on covered plates. Regarding your dinner, sir, well just do what you feel is best and it will all work out.

Exit

LORENZO
O dear discretion, how his words are suited!
The fool hath planted in his memory
An army of good words; and I do know
A many fools, that stand in better place,
Garnish'd like him, that for a tricksy word
Defy the matter. How cheerest thou, Jessica?
And now, good sweet, say thy opinion,
How dost thou like the Lord Bassanio's wife?

I can see that he is very good at playing with words! The fool has in his head An army of useful words, and I know Many fools that are in a better position That know as many words as he does and engage in word play to deflect the subject at hand. How are you, Jessica? Tell me what you think about things— How do you like Lord Bassanio's wife?

JESSICA
Past all expressing. It is very meet
The Lord Bassanio live an upright life;
For, having such a blessing in his lady,
He finds the joys of heaven here on earth;
And if on earth he do not mean it, then
In reason he should never come to heaven
Why, if two gods should play some heavenly match

I like her more than I can say. It is right That Lord Bassanio lives in such an upright way, and by having such a blessing as her in his life he will find more joy here on earth than in heaven. If on this earth with her he can not find happiness He shouldn't even bother going to heaven. Really, if two gods

And on the wager lay two earthly women,
And Portia one, there must be something else
Pawn'd with the other, for the poor rude world
Hath not her fellow.

LORENZO
Even such a husband
Hast thou of me as she is for a wife.

JESSICA
Nay, but ask my opinion too of that.

LORENZO
I will anon: first, let us go to dinner.

JESSICA
Nay, let me praise you while I have a stomach.

LORENZO
No, pray thee, let it serve for table-talk;
' Then, howso'er thou speak'st, 'mong other things
I shall digest it.

JESSICA
Well, I'll set you forth.

Exeunt

were playing a game in heaven And placed a bet on two earthly women with Portia being one of them, there must have been something Lost on the other, for the poor rude world does not contain her equal.

I am as good a husband For you as she is as a wife.

You should ask me about that!

I will later. First, let's go to dinner.

No, let me say good things about you while I feel like it.

No, please, let's talk about it at dinner. That way, no matter what you say, I'll take it in with everything else and digest it.

Well, I'll set you straight about it.

Act IV

SCENE I. Venice. A court of justice.

Enter the DUKE, the Magnificoes, ANTONIO, BASSANIO, GRATIANO, SALERIO, and others

DUKE
What, is Antonio here?

> Is Antonio here?

ANTONIO
Ready, so please your grace.

> Yes, I am here, sir.

DUKE
I am sorry for thee: thou art come to answer
A stony adversary, an inhuman wretch
uncapable of pity, void and empty
From any dram of mercy.

> I feel sorry for you. You've come to face
> A hard enemy, an inhuman wretch
> who is incapable of pity—a man who does
> not have the least amount of mercy.

ANTONIO
I have heard
Your grace hath ta'en great pains to qualify
His rigorous course; but since he stands obdurate
And that no lawful means can carry me
Out of his envy's reach, I do oppose
My patience to his fury, and am arm'd
To suffer, with a quietness of spirit,
The very tyranny and rage of his.

> I've been told
> You have gone to a lot of trouble to try to stop
> What he is planning to do. But since he is so
> stubborn and no legal means can keep me out
> Of his reach, I will face him
> With patience to match his rage. I am ready
> To suffer this quietly
> As he acts out of cruelty and anger.

DUKE
Go one, and call the Jew into the court.

> Someone go tell the Jew to come into the court.

SALERIO
He is ready at the door: he comes, my lord.

> He is waiting at the door. Here he comes.

Enter SHYLOCK

DUKE
Make room, and let him stand before our face.

> Move aside and make room so he can stand before me.

Shylock, the world thinks, and I think so too,
That thou but lead'st this fashion of thy malice

> Shylock, eveyone thinks, and I do, too,
> That even though you have carried on in a hateful way

To the last hour of act; and then 'tis thought

> All the way to the end, it is thought that perhaps

Thou'lt show thy mercy and remorse more strange

> You'll surprise us by showing some mercy and pity

Original	Modern
Than is thy strange apparent cruelty;	Which would be even more remarkable than the obvious cruelty,
And where thou now exact'st the penalty,	And that while you say you will take your penalty—
Which is a pound of this poor merchant's flesh,	Which is a pound of this poor merchant's flead—
Thou wilt not only loose the forfeiture, But, touch'd with human gentleness and love, Forgive a moiety of the principal; Glancing an eye of pity on his losses, That have of late so huddled on his back, Enow to press a royal merchant down And pluck commiseration of his state From brassy bosoms and rough hearts of flint, From stubborn Turks and Tartars, never train'd	You will not only let that go, But, moved to kindness and compassion, You will forgive a portion of the principal, As you look with pity on his losses That have so recently weighed down on him— Enough to drive any merchant down And that would extract feelings of sympathy From the unfeeling and stone-hard hearts Of the most unyielding Turks and Tarters, who were never trained
To offices of tender courtesy. We all expect a gentle answer, Jew.	To offer tenderness or courtesy. We all expect a kind answer, Jew.

SHYLOCK

Original	Modern
I have possess'd your grace of what I purpose; And by our holy Sabbath have I sworn To have the due and forfeit of my bond: If you deny it, let the danger light Upon your charter and your city's freedom. You'll ask me, why I rather choose to have A weight of carrion flesh than to receive Three thousand ducats: I'll not answer that: But, say, it is my humour: is it answer'd?	I have told you that I intend to do What I swear by Holy Sunday to Have the penalty due for the forfeit of the loan. If you deny me that, it will endanger Your city's rights and freedoms. You want to know why I'd rather have A pound of rotting flesh instead of receiving Three thousand ducats. I won't answer that. Let's just say it strikes my fancy— is that enough of an answer?
What if my house be troubled with a rat And I be pleased to give ten thousand ducats To have it baned? What, are you answer'd yet?	What if my house had a rat in it And I wanted to pay ten thousand ducats To have it exterminated? Well, do you have your answer yet?
Some men there are love not a gaping pig;	Some men don't like a roasted pig with its mouth open,
Some, that are mad if they behold a cat; And others, when the bagpipe sings i' the nose,	And others go crazy if they see a cat. Others, when they get a whiff of the sound of bagpipes,
Cannot contain their urine: for affection, Mistress of passion, sways it to the mood	Cannot help but urinate. Our fancy, Which is connected to our most powerful feelings, determines
Of what it likes or loathes. Now, for your answer:	What we like or don't like. So, for your answer:

As there is no firm reason to be render'd, Why he cannot abide a gaping pig; Why he, a harmless necessary cat; Why he, a woollen bagpipe; but of force Must yield to such inevitable shame As to offend, himself being offended; So can I give no reason, nor I will not, More than a lodged hate and a certain loathing I bear Antonio, that I follow thus A losing suit against him. Are you answer'd?	*Just as there is no good reason to be found Why one man cannot stand a roasted pig, And another a harmless and useful cat, And another, the coarse sound of a bagpipe, but who has to yield to a shameful act because he himself is offended— In the same way, I can't give a reason, and I won't, Beyond a deep-rooted hate and a steady loathing for Antonio. So, I will follow through On my claim against him. Do you have your answer?*

BASSANIO
This is no answer, thou unfeeling man, To excuse the current of thy cruelty.	*That is no answer, you heartless man, To excuse how cruel you are being.*

SHYLOCK
I am not bound to please thee with my answers.	*No one said my answers have to please you.*

BASSANIO
Do all men kill the things they do not love?	*Tell me, do all men kill the things they do not love?*

SHYLOCK
Hates any man the thing he would not kill?	*Does any man not want to kill the thing he hates?*

BASSANIO
Every offence is not a hate at first.	*Not every annoyance is hated at first.*

SHYLOCK
What, wouldst thou have a serpent sting thee twice?	*What, would you let a snake bite you twice?*

ANTONIO
I pray you, think you question with the Jew: You may as well go stand upon the beach And bid the main flood bate his usual height; You may as well use question with the wolf Why he hath made the ewe bleat for the lamb; You may as well forbid the mountain pines To wag their high tops and to make no noise, When they are fretten with the gusts of heaven; You may as well do anything most hard, As seek to soften that--than which what's harder?--	*Please, why are you arguing with the Jew? You may as well go stand on the beach And ask the largest waves to decrease in height. You may as well as the wolf Why he killed a lamb and made its mother cry. You may as well tell the pines in the mountains To stop swaying and to be quiet When the wind blows and moves through them. You may as well attempt to do anything just as impossible Than to try to soften his hard*

Original	Modern
His Jewish heart: therefore, I do beseech you, Make no more offers, use no farther means,	Jewish heart. I beg you, Don't make him any more offers, and do try anything else.
But with all brief and plain conveniency Let me have judgment and the Jew his will.	Let's make this brief and as easy as possible— Let me have my punishment and give the Jew what he wants.
BASSANIO For thy three thousand ducats here is six.	Instead of three thousand ducats, here is six.
SHYLOCK If every ducat is six thousand ducats, Were in six parts and every part a ducat, I would not draw them; I would have my bond.	If every ducat were six thousand ducats, And then six times that, I would not have them. I will have my payment.
DUKE How shalt thou hope for mercy, rendering none?	How can you ever hope for mercy when you give none?
SHYLOCK What judgment shall I dread, doing no wrong?	What punishment should I dread, since I do no wrong?
You have among you many a purchased slave,	You have in your possession many slaves you've bought
Which, like your asses and your dogs and mules,	Which—like your donkeys and your dogs and mules—
You use in abject and in slavish parts,	You use to do despicable things just because they are slaves
Because you bought them: shall I say to you, Let them be free, marry them to your heirs?	And you bought them. What if I said to you, 'Set them free and let them marry your children,'
Why sweat they under burthens? let their beds	And 'Why are you making them work so hard?' or 'Give them beds
Be made as soft as yours and let their palates Be season'd with such viands? You will answer	As soft as your and please their palates With the same food you eat?' You would answer,
'The slaves are ours:' so do I answer you: The pound of flesh, which I demand of him, Is dearly bought; 'tis mine and I will have it. If you deny me, fie upon your law! There is no force in the decrees of Venice.	'The slaves are mine.' And so I answer you the same. I demand the pound of flesh— I paid a lot for it. It is mine and I will have it. If you deny me, your laws will mean nothing! You will not be able to enforce the rules of Venice.
I stand for judgment: answer; shall I have it?	I'm waiting for my payment. Answer me: will I have it?
DUKE Upon my power I may dismiss this court,	I will dimiss the court for the day

Unless Bellario, a learned doctor,
Whom I have sent for to determine this,

Come here to-day.

	Unless Bellario, a wise expert of the law
	Whom I sent for to help make the judgement,
	Shows up today.

SALERIO
My lord, here stays without
A messenger with letters from the doctor,
New come from Padua.

Outside there waits
A messenger with letters from the doctor,
Who is arriving from Padua.

DUKE
Bring us the letters; call the messenger.

Bring us the letters and call in the messenger.

BASSANIO
Good cheer, Antonio! What, man, courage yet!
The Jew shall have my flesh, blood, bones and all,

Ere thou shalt lose for me one drop of blood.

Cheer up, Antonio! Keep up your courage!
The Jew can have my flesh, blood, bones—
everything—
Before I let you lose one drop of blood for me.

ANTONIO
I am a tainted wether of the flock,
Meetest for death: the weakest kind of fruit
Drops earliest to the ground; and so let me
You cannot better be employ'd, Bassanio,
Than to live still and write mine epitaph.

I am the diseased sheep in the flock,
Most fit for death. The weakest of the fruit
Falls to the ground first. Let me be the one.
I can't think of a better purpose, Bassanio,
Than for you to live and write my epitaph.

Enter NERISSA, dressed like a lawyer's clerk

DUKE
Came you from Padua, from Bellario?

Have you come from Padua from Bellario's?

NERISSA
From both, my lord. Bellario greets your grace.

From both, sir. Bellario sends his greetings.

Presenting a letter

BASSANIO
Why dost thou whet thy knife so earnestly?

Why are you sharpening your knife so eagerly?

SHYLOCK
To cut the forfeiture from that bankrupt there.

To cut my payment from that bankrupt man over there.

GRATIANO

Not on thy sole, but on thy soul, harsh Jew,	*You shouldn't do it on the sole of your shoe, but on your soul, cruel Jew,*
Thou makest thy knife keen; but no metal can,	*You'd sharpen the knife better than any metal can.*
No, not the hangman's axe, bear half the keenness	*Not even the hangman's ax could be half as sharp*
Of thy sharp envy. Can no prayers pierce thee?	*As the hate inside you. Can no prayers reach you?*

SHYLOCK

No, none that thou hast wit enough to make.	*No, none that you have the intelligence to make.*

GRATIANO

O, be thou damn'd, inexecrable dog!	*Oh, go to hell, you unmovable dog!*
And for thy life let justice be accused.	*You should be killed in the name of justice.*
Thou almost makest me waver in my faith	*You almost cause me to be unsteady in my beliefs,*
To hold opinion with Pythagoras,	*And to agree with the philosopher Pythagoras*
That souls of animals infuse themselves	*That the souls of animals are born again*
Into the boxes of men: thy currish spirit	*As humans. Your dog-like soul*
Govern'd a wolf, who, hang'd for human slaughter,	*Came from a wolf who was slaughtered for killing humans.*
Even from the gallows did his fell soul fleet,	*As he hung from the gallows his savage soul fled*
And, whilst thou lay'st in thy unhallow'd dam,	*And—while you were in the unholy womb of your mother—*
Infused itself in thee; for thy desires	*It came into you. Your desires*
Are wolvish, bloody, starved and ravenous.	*Are wolfish, bloody, starved and insatiable.*

SHYLOCK

Till thou canst rail the seal from off my bond,	*Until you can rant the seal off of my contract,*
Thou but offend'st thy lungs to speak so loud:	*You just hurt your lungs to yell so loudly.*
Repair thy wit, good youth, or it will fall	*Recover your senses, young man, or you will*
To cureless ruin. I stand here for law.	*fall apart. I have the law on my side.*

DUKE

This letter from Bellario doth commend	*This letter from Bellario recommends*
A young and learned doctor to our court.	*A young and well-educated legal expert to our*
Where is he?	*court. Where is he?*

NERISSA

He attendeth here hard by,	*He waits nearby*
To know your answer, whether you'll admit him.	*To hear whether you will admit him into the court.*

DUKE

With all my heart. Some three or four of you	I welcome him with all of my heart. Three or four of you
Go give him courteous conduct to this place. Meantime the court shall hear Bellario's letter.	Go give him a courteous escort here. In the meantime, the court will hear Bellario's letter.

Clerk
[Reads]

Your grace shall understand that at the receipt of your letter I am very sick: but in the instant that your messenger came, in loving visitation was with me a young doctor of Rome; his name is Balthasar. I acquainted him with the cause in controversy between the Jew and Antonio the merchant: we turned o'er many books together: he is furnished with my opinion; which, bettered with his own learning, the greatness whereof I cannot enough commend, comes with him, at my importunity, to fill up your grace's request in my stead. I beseech you, let his lack of years be no impediment to let him lack a reverend estimation; for I never knew so young a body with so old a head. I leave him to your gracious acceptance, whose trial shall better publish his commendation.	[Reads] Please understand that even though I received your letter, I am very ill at the time. However, when your messenger delivered the letter, I was being visited by a young doctor from Rome whose name is Balthasar. I told him about the controvery regarding the Jew and Antonio the merchant. We looked over many books together. He is aware of my opinion on the matter, which was made better with his knowledge, which is so broad I could not recommend him more, and he brings my opinion with him, since I am not able to do so, and will fill your request in place of me. Please do not let his young age fool you into thinking he is not worthy of respect and high esteem. I've never known such a young body graced with such a wise head. I leave him for you to accept into court. Once you see what he can do, he will commend himself by his actions.

DUKE

You hear the learn'd Bellario, what he writes: And here, I take it, is the doctor come.	You hear the wise Bellario has written. And here comes the expert he recommends.

Enter PORTIA, dressed like a doctor of laws

Give me your hand. Come you from old Bellario?	Please, shake my hand. Have you come from Bellario?

PORTIA

I did, my lord.	I did, sir.

DUKE

You are welcome: take your place. Are you acquainted with the difference That holds this present question in the court?	Welcome, and please take a seat. Are you acquainted with the case That is currently before the court?

PORTIA

I am informed thoroughly of the cause.
Which is the merchant here, and which the Jew?

DUKE
Antonio and old Shylock, both stand forth.

PORTIA
Is your name Shylock?

SHYLOCK
Shylock is my name.

PORTIA
Of a strange nature is the suit you follow;
Yet in such rule that the Venetian law
Cannot impugn you as you do proceed.
You stand within his danger, do you not?

ANTONIO
Ay, so he says.

PORTIA
Do you confess the bond?

ANTONIO
I do.

PORTIA
Then must the Jew be merciful.

SHYLOCK
On what compulsion must I? tell me that.

PORTIA *"Quality of Mercy"*
The quality of mercy is not strain'd,
It droppeth as the gentle rain from heaven
Upon the place beneath: it is twice blest;
It blesseth him that gives and him that takes:
'Tis mightiest in the mightiest: it becomes
The throned monarch better than his crown;
His sceptre shows the force of temporal power,
The attribute to awe and majesty,

Wherein doth sit the dread and fear of kings;

I am thoroughly familiar with the case.
Which is the merchant, here, and which is the Jew?

Antonio and Shylock, please step forward.

Is your name Shylock?

My name is Shylock.

The case you present is very strange,
Yet is so valid that the Venetian law
Cannot dispute it as you go forward with it.
You stand within danger here, don't you?

Yes, that's what he says.

Do you acknowledge the contract?

I do.

Then the Jew must show mercy.

Why should I do that? Tell me.

Mercy is not something that can be forced.
It drops like soft rain from heaven
Upon the place beneath it. It twice blesses:
It blesses he who gives it and he who receives it. It is influential in the most influential people. It makes a king look better than his own crown does. His scepter shows his power and strength on earth, It is a credit to his awe and grandness.
Within it sits the dread and fear of kings,

But mercy is above this sceptred sway; It is enthroned in the hearts of kings, It is an attribute to God himself; And earthly power doth then show likest God's When mercy seasons justice. Therefore, Jew, Though justice be thy plea, consider this, That, in the course of justice, none of us Should see salvation: we do pray for mercy; And that same prayer doth teach us all to render The deeds of mercy. I have spoke thus much To mitigate the justice of thy plea; Which if thou follow, this strict court of Venice Must needs give sentence 'gainst the merchant there.	But mercy has more power and is higher than the scepter. It is enthroned within the hearts of kings. It is a credit to God himself, Earthly power seems most like God's power When mercy is added to justice. So, Jew, Although it is justice you want, consider this. Following the course of justice alone won't save you. We pray for mercy, And saying the prayer teaches us to give mercy. I have said all of this To persuade you to reduce the severity of your claim, Which, if you follow through, this strict court of Venice Will have to serve sentence against the merchant there.

SHYLOCK

My deeds upon my head! I crave the law, The penalty and forfeit of my bond.	My actions are my own! I want the law— The payment for the forfeit of the contract.

PORTIA

Is he not able to discharge the money?	Can't he the contract just be dimissed with payment?

BASSANIO

Yes, here I tender it for him in the court; Yea, twice the sum: if that will not suffice, I will be bound to pay it ten times o'er, On forfeit of my hands, my head, my heart: If this will not suffice, it must appear That malice bears down truth. And I beseech you, Wrest once the law to your authority: To do a great right, do a little wrong, And curb this cruel devil of his will.	Yes, I'm willing to give it to him right here in the court. Yes, even twice the amount, and if that is not enough I will sign a contract to pay it ten times over, And will give up my hands, my head, my heart: If that is not enough, it would seem You are just truly evil. I beg you, Just once take the law into your authority— Do a great right by doing a little wrong, And keep this devil from getting what he wants.

PORTIA

It must not be; there is no power in Venice Can alter a decree established: 'Twill be recorded for a precedent, And many an error by the same example Will rush into the state: it cannot be.	No, that can't be. There is no power in Venice That can alter a law once it is established. It will be recorded as a precedent And many errors will occur by example As others rush in after it: it cannot be.

SHYLOCK

A Daniel come to judgment! yea, a Daniel!
O wise young judge, how I do honour thee!

PORTIA
I pray you, let me look upon the bond.

SHYLOCK
Here 'tis, most reverend doctor, here it is.

PORTIA
Shylock, there's thrice thy money offer'd thee.

SHYLOCK
An oath, an oath, I have an oath in heaven:

Shall I lay perjury upon my soul?
No, not for Venice.

PORTIA
Why, this bond is forfeit;
And lawfully by this the Jew may claim
A pound of flesh, to be by him cut off
Nearest the merchant's heart. Be merciful:

Take thrice thy money; bid me tear the bond.

SHYLOCK
When it is paid according to the tenor.

It doth appear you are a worthy judge;
You know the law, your exposition
Hath been most sound: I charge you by the law,

Whereof you are a well-deserving pillar,

Proceed to judgment: by my soul I swear
There is no power in the tongue of man
To alter me: I stay here on my bond.

ANTONIO
Most heartily I do beseech the court
To give the judgment.

PORTIA

A fine judge has come to judge! Yes, a Daniel!
Oh, wise young judge—I do applaude you!

Please, let me look at the contract.

Here it is, most respected expert, here it is.

Shylock, they are offering you three times the amount you lent.

But I made an oath! I made an oath by heaven!
Should I have a false oath upon my soul?
No, not for Venice.

Well, this contract is forfeited.
And, by law, this Jew may claim
A pound of flesh to be cut off by him
Nearest the merchant's heart. But I'm asking you to show mercy:
Take three times the money, and let me tear up the contract.

It can be torn up when it is paid according to its content.

You do appear to be a worthy judge.
You know the law well, and your argument
Has been very solid. I command you by the law—
Of which you are a well-deserving support of—
To make your judgement. By my soul I swear
The is nothing anyone can say
That will change my mind. I wait here for my payment.

Please, I beg the court
To give the judgement.

Why then, thus it is:
You must prepare your bosom for his knife.

SHYLOCK
O noble judge! O excellent young man!

PORTIA
For the intent and purpose of the law
Hath full relation to the penalty,
Which here appeareth due upon the bond.

SHYLOCK
'Tis very true: O wise and upright judge!
How much more elder art thou than thy looks!

PORTIA
Therefore lay bare your bosom.
SHYLOCK
Ay, his breast:
So says the bond: doth it not, noble judge?
'Nearest his heart:' those are the very words.

PORTIA
It is so. Are there balance here to weigh
The flesh?

SHYLOCK
I have them ready.

PORTIA
Have by some surgeon, Shylock, on your charge,
To stop his wounds, lest he do bleed to death.

SHYLOCK
Is it so nominated in the bond?

PORTIA
It is not so express'd: but what of that?
'Twere good you do so much for charity.

SHYLOCK
I cannot find it; 'tis not in the bond.

PORTIA

Well then, so it is:
You must perpare your chest for his knife.

Oh, noble judge! Oh, excellent young man!

The law fully supports
The penalty
Which is written in the contract.

It's very true! Oh wise and upright judge!
You seem much older thatn you look!

So, you must lay bare your chest.

Yes, his chest:
That's what the contract says, doesn't it, good
judge? 'Nearest his heart.' Those are the ords.

That is right. Is there a balance here to weight
The flesh?

I have it ready.

Get a surgeon, Shylock, that you will pay
To attend to his wounds and keep him from
bleeding to death.

Does it say that in the contract?

It is not written in it, but so what?
It would be good for you to show the charity.

I cannot find it—it is not in the contract.

You, merchant, have you any thing to say?	You, merchant, do you have anything to say?
ANTONIO But little: I am arm'd and well prepared.	I don't have much to say. I am ready and prepared.
Give me your hand, Bassanio: fare you well! Grieve not that I am fallen to this for you; For herein Fortune shows herself more kind Than is her custom: it is still her use To let the wretched man outlive his wealth,	Give me your hand, Bassanio: goodbye! Don't be sad that I have fallen like this for you Because Fortune is showing herself to be kinder than is her custom. She usually lets The man who has fallen low to outlive his wealth,
To view with hollow eye and wrinkled brow	And to view with an empty eye and a wrinkled forehead
An age of poverty; from which lingering penance Of such misery doth she cut me off.	The poverty that has set in, but as far as the lingering suffering and misery—Fortune has ended it.
Commend me to your honourable wife: Tell her the process of Antonio's end;	Speak well of me to your honorable wife. Tell her what happened to bring about my end,
Say how I loved you, speak me fair in death;	And tell her I loved you, and speak well of me after I am gone.
And, when the tale is told, bid her be judge Whether Bassanio had not once a love. Repent but you that you shall lose your friend, And he repents not that he pays your debt; For if the Jew do cut but deep enough, I'll pay it presently with all my heart.	And when the story is told, allow her to be the judge of whether Bassinio once has a friend. Only feel sorry that you will lose your friend, And know he doesn't feel sorry to pay your debt. If the Jew cuts deep enough I will soon pay for it with all of my heart.
BASSANIO Antonio, I am married to a wife Which is as dear to me as life itself; But life itself, my wife, and all the world, Are not with me esteem'd above thy life: I would lose all, ay, sacrifice them all Here to this devil, to deliver you.	Antonio, I have a wife Who is as dear to me as life itself. But life itself, my wife, and all the world Are not more important than your life. I would lose it all—yes—sacrifice them all To this devil, if I could save you.
PORTIA Your wife would give you little thanks for that, If she were by, to hear you make the offer.	Your wife might not be hapy to hear that, If she were here to hear you make that offer.
GRATIANO I have a wife, whom, I protest, I love: I would she were in heaven, so she could	I have a wife whom I love very much. If she were in heaven, she could

Original	Modern
Entreat some power to change this currish Jew.	Ask some heavenly power to change the mind of this dog Jew.
NERISSA 'Tis well you offer it behind her back; The wish would make else an unquiet house.	It's good you offer it behind her back. This wish would make for an argument at home.
SHYLOCK These be the Christian husbands. I have a daughter; Would any of the stock of Barrabas Had been her husband rather than a Christian!	That's what you get with Christian husbands. I have a daughter. I'd rather any descendent of Barrabas Would have been her husband instead of a Christian!
Aside We trifle time: I pray thee, pursue sentence.	We waste time. Please, carry on with the sentence.
PORTIA A pound of that same merchant's flesh is thine: The court awards it, and the law doth give it.	A pound of this merchant's flesh is yours— The court awards it, and the law will give it to you.
SHYLOCK Most rightful judge!	You are a just judge!
PORTIA And you must cut this flesh from off his breast: The law allows it, and the court awards it.	And you must cut this flesh off of his chest. The law allows for it, and the court awards it.
SHYLOCK Most learned judge! A sentence! Come, prepare!	You are an educatied judge! A sentence! Come on, let's get ready!
PORTIA Tarry a little; there is something else. This bond doth give thee here no jot of blood; The words expressly are 'a pound of flesh:' Take then thy bond, take thou thy pound of flesh; But, in the cutting it, if thou dost shed One drop of Christian blood, thy lands and goods Are, by the laws of Venice, confiscate Unto the state of Venice.	Wait a minute. There is something else. This contract says that there should not be a spot of blood, The words say exactly 'a pound of flesh.' So, take your payment, and take your pound of flesh. But if, in cutting it, your shed One drop of Christian blood, your land and property are, by the law of Venice, confiscated To the state of Venice.
GRATIANO O upright judge! Mark, Jew: O learned judge!	Oh, good judge! Listen, Jew! Oh, educated judge!
SHYLOCK	

Is that the law?	*Is that the law?*
PORTIA Thyself shalt see the act: For, as thou urgest justice, be assured Thou shalt have justice, more than thou desirest.	*You can look at it for yourself.* *You have asked for justice, and—rest assured—* *You will have more justice than you desired.*
GRATIANO O learned judge! Mark, Jew: a learned judge!	*Oh, educated judge! Listen, Jew—an educated judge!*
SHYLOCK I take this offer, then; pay the bond thrice And let the Christian go.	*I will take your offer, then. Pay the principle three times over and let the Christian go free.*
BASSANIO Here is the money.	*Here is the money.*
PORTIA Soft! The Jew shall have all justice; soft! no haste: He shall have nothing but the penalty.	*Wait!* *The Jew wants justice. Wait! Don't hurry.* *He will have nothing but his payment.*
GRATIANO O Jew! an upright judge, a learned judge!	*Oh, Jew! A good judge! An educated judge!*
PORTIA Therefore prepare thee to cut off the flesh. Shed thou no blood, nor cut thou less nor more But just a pound of flesh: if thou cut'st more Or less than a just pound, be it but so much As makes it light or heavy in the substance, Or the division of the twentieth part Of one poor scruple, nay, if the scale do turn But in the estimation of a hair, Thou diest and all thy goods are confiscate.	*So, prepare to cut off the flesh.* *Be careful not to shed any blood, or to cut more or less* *Than exactly a pound of flesh. If you cut more* *Or less than a pound—be it so little as* *to makes it lighter or heavier in weight* *by a twentieth of a part,* *Even one ounce, if the scale shows* *But the weight of a hair—* *You die and all of your property will be confiscated.*
GRATIANO A second Daniel, a Daniel, Jew! Now, infidel, I have you on the hip.	*A second Daniel! A very fair judge, Jew!* *Not, you who have no faith, I am one up on you.*
PORTIA	

Why doth the Jew pause? take thy forfeiture.

SHYLOCK
Give me my principal, and let me go.

BASSANIO
I have it ready for thee; here it is.

PORTIA
He hath refused it in the open court:
He shall have merely justice and his bond.

GRATIANO
A Daniel, still say I, a second Daniel!

I thank thee, Jew, for teaching me that word.

SHYLOCK
Shall I not have barely my principal?

PORTIA
Thou shalt have nothing but the forfeiture,
To be so taken at thy peril, Jew.

SHYLOCK
Why, then the devil give him good of it!
I'll stay no longer question.

PORTIA
Tarry, Jew: *"Tarry Jew"*
The law hath yet another hold on you.
It is enacted in the laws of Venice,
If it be proved against an alien
That by direct or indirect attempts
He seek the life of any citizen,
The party 'gainst the which he doth contrive
Shall seize one half his goods; the other half
Comes to the privy coffer of the state;
And the offender's life lies in the mercy
Of the duke only, 'gainst all other voice.
In which predicament, I say, thou stand'st;
For it appears, by manifest proceeding,
That indirectly and directly too
Thou hast contrived against the very life

Why do you hesitate, Jew? Take your payment.

Give me my principal, and I will go.

I have it ready for you. Here it is.

He refused it in the open court.
He only wants justice and to have his payment.

A fair judge, again, I'm saying! A second Daniel!
Thank you, Jew, for teaching me that phrase.

So, I don't even get my principal?

You will have nothing but the forfeiture,
Which will be taken at your risk, Jew.

Well, then the devil gives it to him!
I won't stay here any longer.

Wait a minute, Jew.
The law still has a hold on you.
It is written in the laws of Venice
That if it shown a foreigner,
By direct or indirect attempts,
Tries to take the life of a citizen of Venice,
The person he tried to take the life of
Is entitled to one half of his propery, and the other half goes to the state.
The offender's life lies in the mercy
Of the duke, and only the duke.
This seems to be your situation.
It appears so, by clear course of action
That you indirectly and directly taken.
You have plotted against the life

Of the defendant; and thou hast incurr'd	Of the defendant, and you have, by your actions,
The danger formerly by me rehearsed.	Brought on the harm to yourself I previously mentioned.
Down therefore and beg mercy of the duke.	So, get down on your knees, then, and beg mercy of the duke.

GRATIANO

Beg that thou mayst have leave to hang thyself:	Beg that you may be allowed to hang yourself
And yet, thy wealth being forfeit to the state,	But, if your wealth goes to the state,
Thou hast not left the value of a cord;	You won't have enough money to buy a rope,
Therefore thou must be hang'd at the state's charge.	And you will have to be hung at cost to the state.

DUKE

That thou shalt see the difference of our spirits,	I want you to see the difference between our temperments.
I pardon thee thy life before thou ask it:	I pardon your life before you ask for it.
For half thy wealth, it is Antonio's;	Half of your wealth goes to Antonio.
The other half comes to the general state,	The other half goes to the state.
Which humbleness may drive unto a fine.	If you show humility, I may drop that to a fine.

PORTIA

Ay, for the state, not for Antonio.	The state's half can be dropped, but not Antonio's.

SHYLOCK

Nay, take my life and all;	No, go ahead and take my life with all of it.
pardon not that:	Don't pardon that.
You take my house when you do take the prop	You take my house when your take the income
That doth sustain my house; you take my life	That keeps my house. You take my life
When you do take the means whereby I live.	When you take away the place where I live.

PORTIA

What mercy can you render him, Antonio?	Can you show him any mercy, Antonio?

GRATIANO

A halter gratis; nothing else, for God's sake.	Give him a rope to hang himself free of charge, for God's sake!

ANTONIO

So please my lord the duke and all the court	If the duke and the courst
To quit the fine for one half of his goods,	Drop the fine for one half of his property
I am content; so he will let me have	I am satisfied, as long as he will allow
The other half in use, to render it,	The other half to be put in trust
Upon his death, unto the gentleman	So that when he dies, it will go to the man
That lately stole his daughter:	Who recently stole his daughter.

Original	Modern
Two things provided more, that, for this favour,	And two more things: that he, due to this favor being granted,
He presently become a Christian;	Immediatley becomes a Christian.
The other, that he do record a gift,	The other is that is records a will,
Here in the court, of all he dies possess'd,	Here in this court, that gives all when he dies
Unto his son Lorenzo and his daughter.	To his son-in-law Lorenzo and his daughter.

DUKE

He shall do this, or else I do recant	He will do this or else I will take back
The pardon that I late pronounced here.	The pardon I just gave to him.

PORTIA

Art thou contented, Jew? what dost thou say?	Are you happy with that, Jew? What do you say?

SHYLOCK

I am content.	I am happy with that.

PORTIA

Clerk, draw a deed of gift.	Clerk, make up a deed of gift for him to sign.

SHYLOCK

I pray you, give me leave to go from hence;	Please, allow me to leave now,
I am not well: send the deed after me,	I am not feeling well. Send the deed after me
And I will sign it.	And I will sign it.

DUKE

Get thee gone, but do it.	Go on, then, but be sure to sign the deed.

GRATIANO

In christening shalt thou have two god-fathers:	When you are christened you will have two god-fathers.
Had I been judge, thou shouldst have had ten more,	If I had been the judge, you would have had ten more,
To bring thee to the gallows, not the font.	As jurors that would bring you to the gallows, and not to be baptized.

Exit SHYLOCK

DUKE

Sir, I entreat you home with me to dinner.	Sir, please come to my house for dinner.

PORTIA

I humbly do desire your grace of pardon:	I humbly do request your pardon.
I must away this night toward Padua,	I must leave tonight to go to Padua,
And it is meet I presently set forth.	And it is urgent that I leave immediatley.

DUKE
I am sorry that your leisure serves you not.
Antonio, gratify this gentleman,
For, in my mind, you are much bound to him.

I am sorry you don't have the time to join me. Antonio, you should reward this gentleman. In my mind, you are very much in debt to him.

Exeunt Duke and his train

BASSANIO
Most worthy gentleman, I and my friend
Have by your wisdom been this day acquitted
Of grievous penalties; in lieu whereof,
Three thousand ducats, due unto the Jew,
We freely cope your courteous pains withal.

Sir, my friend and I Have been aquitted today due to your wisdom From serious penalties. We'd like to give you The three thousand ducats that were due the Jew as recompense for the pains you have taken on our behalf.

ANTONIO
And stand indebted, over and above,
In love and service to you evermore.

We would still be indebted to you, And owe you love and service forever.

PORTIA
He is well paid that is well satisfied;
And I, delivering you, am satisfied
And therein do account myself well paid:
My mind was never yet more mercenary.
I pray you, know me when we meet again:
I wish you well, and so I take my leave.

He who does a good job is well paid, And I, in freeing you, am sastified And I consider myself well paid in that alone. I wasn't thinking about money. I hope you recognize me when we meet again. I wish you the best. I'm going to go, now.

BASSANIO
Dear sir, of force I must attempt you further:
Take some remembrance of us, as a tribute,
Not as a fee: grant me two things, I pray you,
Not to deny me, and to pardon me.

Sir, I must insist you Take some token from us, as a gift, Not as a payment. Please grant me two things: Don't say no, and forgive me for insisting.

PORTIA
You press me far, and therefore I will yield.

You insist so much, and so I will give in and accept.

To ANTONIO
Give me your gloves, I'll wear them for your sake;

Give me your gloves. I will wear them for your sake.

To BASSANIO
And, for your love, I'll take this ring from you:
Do not draw back your hand; I'll take no more;
And you in love shall not deny me this.

And from you, I'll take this ring. Don't pull back your hand—I'll have nothing else. You can't deny me this gift.

BASSANIO
This ring, good sir, alas, it is a trifle!
I will not shame myself to give you this.

PORTIA
I will have nothing else but only this;
And now methinks I have a mind to it.

BASSANIO
There's more depends on this than on the value.

The dearest ring in Venice will I give you,

And find it out by proclamation:
Only for this, I pray you, pardon me.

PORTIA
I see, sir, you are liberal in offers
You taught me first to beg; and now methinks
You teach me how a beggar should be answer'd.

BASSANIO
Good sir, this ring was given me by my wife;
And when she put it on, she made me vow

That I should neither sell nor give nor lose it.

PORTIA
That 'scuse serves many men to save their gifts.

An if your wife be not a mad-woman,
And know how well I have deserved the ring,

She would not hold out enemy for ever,
For giving it to me. Well, peace be with you!
Exeunt Portia and Nerissa

ANTONIO
My Lord Bassanio, let him have the ring:
Let his deservings and my love withal
Be valued against your wife's commandment.

BASSANIO
Go, Gratiano, run and overtake him;

---

*But this ring, sir, it's nothing!
I would be ashamed to give you this.*

*I will having nothing else but the ring.
Now that I think about it, I really want it.*

*This ring means more to me than its actual value.
I will give you the most expensive ring in Venice,
And put out a public announcement to find it.
But please forgive me for not giving you this ring.*

*I see, sir, that you make big offers.
You taught me how to beg, and now it seems
You are teaching me how a beggar should be answered.*

*Sir, this ring was given to me by my wife,
And when she put it on my finger she made me promise
That I should never sell it or give it away or lose it.*

*Many men use that excuse as a reason not to give things away.
If your wife is not a madwoman,
And you told her how much I did to deserve the ring,
She would not be mad at you forever
For giving it to me. Well, goodbye.*

*Lord Bassanio, let him have the ring.
Consider how much he deserves and my
Friendship against your wife's order.*

Go, Gratianio—run after him

Give him the ring, and bring him, if thou canst, Unto Antonio's house: away! make haste.	*Give him the ring and bring him, if you can,* *To Antonio's house. Hurry! Run after him!*

Exit Gratiano

Come, you and I will thither presently; And in the morning early will we both Fly toward Belmont: come, Antonio.	*Come on, you and I will go now,* *And early tomorrow morning we will both* *Hurry to get to Belmont. Come on, Antonio.*

Exeunt

SCENE II. The same. A street.

Enter PORTIA and NERISSA

PORTIA
Inquire the Jew's house out, give him this deed

And let him sign it: we'll away to-night
And be a day before our husbands home:
This deed will be well welcome to Lorenzo.

Enter GRATIANO

GRATIANO
Fair sir, you are well o'erta'en
My Lord Bassanio upon more advice
Hath sent you here this ring, and doth entreat
Your company at dinner.

PORTIA
That cannot be:
His ring I do accept most thankfully:
And so, I pray you, tell him: furthermore,
I pray you, show my youth old Shylock's house.

GRATIANO
That will I do.

NERISSA
Sir, I would speak with you.

Aside to PORTIA
I'll see if I can get my husband's ring,
Which I did make him swear to keep for ever.

PORTIA
[Aside to NERISSA] Thou mayst, I warrant.
We shall have old swearing
That they did give the rings away to men;
But we'll outface them, and outswear them too.

Aloud

Away! make haste:

Ask where the Jew's house is, then give him this deed
And have him sign it. We'll leave tonight
And be home a day before our husbands.
Lorenzo will be happy to see this deed.

Sir, it's a good thing I caught up with you.
Bassanio took my advice
And has sent me after you with this ring. He requests your company at dinner tonight.

We can't do that.
I accept his ring with much gratitude,
So please tell him that. Also,
Can you show this young man to Shylock's house?

I will do that.

Sir, may I speak with you?

I'll see if I can get my husband's ring,
Which I made him swear to keep forever.

[Aside to NERISSA] I bet you will be able to.
They will swear to us
That they gave the rings to men,
But we will confront then and swear more than them.

Go on! Hurry.

thou knowist where I will tarry.   *You know where I will be.*
NERISSA
Come, good sir, will you show me to this house?   *Come, sir, will you show me to his house?*

Exeunt

Act V

SCENE I. Belmont. Avenue to PORTIA'S house.

Enter LORENZO and JESSICA

LORENZO
The moon shines bright: in such a night as this,

When the sweet wind did gently kiss the trees
And they did make no noise, in such a night
Troilus methinks mounted the Troyan walls
And sigh'd his soul toward the Grecian tents,
Where Cressid lay that night.

JESSICA
In such a night
Did Thisbe fearfully o'ertrip the dew
And saw the lion's shadow ere himself
And ran dismay'd away.

LORENZO
In such a night
Stood Dido with a willow in her hand
Upon the wild sea banks and waft her love
To come again to Carthage.

JESSICA
In such a night
Medea gather'd the enchanted herbs
That did renew old Aeson.

LORENZO
In such a night
Did Jessica steal from the wealthy Jew
And with an unthrift love did run from Venice
As far as Belmont.

JESSICA
In such a night
Did young Lorenzo swear he loved her well,

Stealing her soul with many vows of faith
And ne'er a true one.

LORENZO

The moon shines so brightly tonight. On a night like this,
When the wind blows so gently in the treetops
They barely make noise—on a night just like this, I think Troilus climbed the Troyan walls
And sighed toward the Grecian tents
Where his love Cressida slept.

On a night like this
Thisbe tripped over the dew
When he saw the lion's shadow before him
And ran away in fear.

On a night like this,
Dido stood with a willow branch in her hand
On the wild seashore and signaled her lover
To come back to Carthage.

On a night like this,
Medea gathered the magic herbs
That rejuvenated old Aeson.

On a night like this,
Jessica stole from the wealthy Jew
And with her spendthrift lover
All the way to Belmont.

On a night like this
Young Lorenzo swore he loved Jessica very much
And won her soul with many vows of love,
But not one single vow was true.

In such a night
Did pretty Jessica, like a little shrew,
Slander her love, and he forgave it her.

JESSICA
I would out-night you, did no body come;
But, hark, I hear the footing of a man.

Enter STEPHANO

LORENZO
Who comes so fast in silence of the night?

STEPHANO
A friend.

LORENZO
A friend! what friend?
your name, I pray you, friend?

STEPHANO
Stephano is my name; and I bring word

My mistress will before the break of day
Be here at Belmont; she doth stray about
By holy crosses, where she kneels and prays

For happy wedlock hours.

LORENZO
Who comes with her?

STEPHANO
None but a holy hermit and her maid.
I pray you, is my master yet return'd?

LORENZO
He is not, nor we have not heard from him.
But go we in, I pray thee, Jessica,
And ceremoniously let us prepare
Some welcome for the mistress of the house.

Enter LAUNCELOT

---

*On a night like this,
Pretty Jessica, like a troublesome person,
Said awful things about her lover, and he forgave her.*

I would outdo you if making references to the night if nobody came, But, listen, I hear footsteps.

Who comes so quickly in the quiet of night?

A friend.

*A friend! What friend?
What is your name, please, friend?*

*My name is Stephano, and I am here to tell you
My mistress will be here before the sun rises,
Back in Belmont. She's still among
The holy crosses at the monastery, where she's on her knees praying
For a happy marriage.*

Who is coming with her?

*Just a holy hermit and her maid.
Tell me, has my master returned yet?*

*He's not here, and we haven't heard from him
But let's go inside, Jessica,
And prepare a ceremony
To welcome the mistress back to her house.*

LAUNCELOT
Sola, sola! wo ha, ho! sola, sola!

Hello! Hello! Wo, ha, ho! Hello! Hello!

LORENZO
Who calls?

Who's shouting?

LAUNCELOT
Sola! did you see Master Lorenzo?
Master Lorenzo, sola, sola!

Hello! Did you see Master Lorenzo? Master Lorenzo! Hello! Hello!

LORENZO
Leave hollaing, man: here.

Stop the hollering, man, I'm here.

LAUNCELOT
Sola! where? where?

Hello! Where? Where?

LORENZO
Here.

Here.

LAUNCELOT
Tell him there's a post come from my master, with his horn full of good news: my master will be here ere morning.

Tell him a message has arrived from my master, full of very good news. My master will be here before morning.

Exit

LORENZO
Sweet soul, let's in, and there expect their coming.
And yet no matter: why should we go in?
My friend Stephano, signify, I pray you,
Within the house, your mistress is at hand;
And bring your music forth into the air.

Sweethear, let's go in and wait for them to arrive. But, waiy, it doesn't matter—why should we go in? Friend Stephano, please make it known inside the house that your mistress is coming, and bring muscians out here.

Exit Stephano

How sweet the moonlight sleeps upon this bank!

Here will we sit and let the sounds of music
Creep in our ears: soft stillness and the night
Become the touches of sweet harmony.
Sit, Jessica. Look how the floor of heaven

Is thick inlaid with patines of bright gold:
There's not the smallest orb which thou behold'st

See how lovely the moonlight looks on the bank!
Let's sit here and let the sounds of music Creep into our ears. The stillness of nightime Makes the music all the more sweet sounding. Sit down, Jessica. Look at how the floor of heaven
Is inlaid with a thin layer of bright gold: Even the smallest star that you can see

But in his motion like an angel sings, Still quiring to the young-eyed cherubins; Such harmony is in immortal souls; But whilst this muddy vesture of decay Doth grossly close it in, we cannot hear it. *Enter Musicians* Come, ho! and wake Diana with a hymn! With sweetest touches pierce your mistress' ear, And draw her home with music.	*Sings like an angel in its motion, Silently choiring to the youthful cherubs. Immortal beings can hear the songs, But we who live here on earth And live in earthly bodies cannot hear it.* *Come on! Wake Diana with a song! With the sweetest touches play your instruments so your mistress can hear And bring her home with music.*

Music

JESSICA
I am never merry when I hear sweet music.

LORENZO
The reason is, your spirits are attentive:

For do but note a wild and wanton herd,
Or race of youthful and unhandled colts,
Fetching mad bounds,
bellowing and neighing loud,
Which is the hot condition of their blood;
If they but hear perchance a trumpet sound,

Or any air of music touch their ears,

You shall perceive them make a mutual stand,
Their savage eyes turn'd to a modest gaze
By the sweet power of music: therefore the poet

Did feign that Orpheus drew trees,
stones and floods;
Since nought so stockish, hard and full of rage,

But music for the time doth change his nature.
The man that hath no music in himself,
Nor is not moved with concord of sweet sounds,

Is fit for treasons, stratagems and spoils;
The motions of his spirit are dull as night
And his affections dark as Erebus:

I never feel like laughing when I hear sweet music.

That's because your feelings are paying attention to the music.
Think about a frolicking herd of wild animals,
Or a herd of young and untrained colts,
Jumping around like crazy,
bellowing and neighing loudly,
Which is how they are naturally,
But if they happen to hear the sound of a trumpet,
Or if the sound of soft music touches their ears,
You will see them all stop and stand still—
Their wild eyes calming
From the power of the music. That is why the poet
Wrote how Orpheus could bring trees,
stones and rivers to him with music,
There is not much in the world too stupid,
hard or full of anger
That can not be changed by music.
The man that has no music in him—
Who is not moved by the harmony of sweet sounds—
Is only good for betrayal, schemes and ruin.
His soul is as dull as the night,
And his emotions are dark as the son of Chaos.

Let no such man be trusted. Mark the music.	*A man like that can not be trusted. Listen to the music.*
Enter PORTIA and NERISSA	
PORTIA That light we see is burning in my hall. How far that little candle throws his beams! So shines a good deed in a naughty world.	*That light we see in burning in my house. Look how far that candle throws its beams! That's how a good deed shines in an evil world.*
NERISSA When the moon shone, we did not see the candle.	*When the moon was shining, we did not see the candle.*
PORTIA So doth the greater glory dim the less: A substitute shines brightly as a king Unto the king be by, and then his state Empties itself, as doth an inland brook Into the main of waters. Music! hark!	*Brighter lights always dim the less. Antoher light shines as brightly as a king Until the king comes along, and then the other light Suddenly becomes less, in the same way an inland stream empties into the sea. Music! Listen!*
NERISSA It is your music, madam, of the house.	*It is your music, madam, coming from your house.*
PORTIA Nothing is good, I see, without respect: Methinks it sounds much sweeter than by day.	*I see now that you can't consider anything good without comparison. I think music sounds sweeter at night than during the day.*
NERISSA Silence bestows that virtue on it, madam.	*The quiet of night gives it that quality, madam.*
PORTIA The crow doth sing as sweetly as the lark, When neither is attended, and I think The nightingale, if she should sing by day, When every goose is cackling, would be thought No better a musician than the wren. How many things by season season'd are To their right praise and true perfection! Peace, ho! the moon sleeps with Endymion And would not be awaked.	*The crow sings as sweetly as the lark does When neither is listened to. I think The nightingale—if it were to sing by day, When all the geese are cackling—would be no better regarded As a musician than the common wren. How many things are made to seem right and praised as perfect if they come at the right time! Quiet, now! The moon sleeps with its lover Endymion and will not be awoken.*

Music ceases

LORENZO
That is the voice,
Or I am much deceived, of Portia.
PORTIA
He knows me as the blind man knows the cuckoo,
By the bad voice.

LORENZO
Dear lady, welcome home.

PORTIA
We have been praying for our husbands' healths,
Which speed, we hope, the better for our words.
Are they return'd?

LORENZO
Madam, they are not yet;
But there is come a messenger before,
To signify their coming.

PORTIA
Go in, Nerissa;
Give order to my servants that they take
No note at all of our being absent hence;
Nor you, Lorenzo; Jessica, nor you.

A tucket sounds

LORENZO
Your husband is at hand; I hear his trumpet:
We are no tell-tales, madam; fear you not.

PORTIA
This night methinks is but the daylight sick;
It looks a little paler: 'tis a day,
Such as the day is when the sun is hid.

Enter BASSANIO, ANTONIO, GRATIANO, and their followers

BASSANIO
We should hold day with the Antipodes,
If you would walk in absence of the sun.

---

*That is the voice
of Portia, if I am not mistaken.*

*He recognizes me like the blind man
recognizes the cuckoo— by its bad voice.*

Dear lady, welcome home.

*We have been praying for our husbands'
health. We hope they are better off for our
words. Have they come back, yet?*

*Madam, they are not back yet.
But a messenger came earlier
And said they are on their way.*

*Go inside, Nerissa.
Tell the servants they must not mention
That we have been gone.
You neither, Lorenzo, or you, Jessica.*

*Your husband is here—I hear his trumpet
We are not tattle-tales, madam, don't worry.*

*I think this night looks like sick daylight.
It looks a little paler. It's like a day
When the sun is hidden.*

*It is daylight on the other side of the world,
While you walk here at night.*

PORTIA
Let me give light, but let me not be light;

For a light wife doth make a heavy husband,

And never be Bassanio so for me:

But God sort all! You are welcome home, my lord.

BASSANIO
I thank you, madam. Give welcome to my friend.

This is the man, this is Antonio,
To whom I am so infinitely bound.

PORTIA
You should in all sense be much bound to him.

For, as I hear, he was much bound for you.

ANTONIO
No more than I am well acquitted of.

PORTIA
Sir, you are very welcome to our house:
It must appear in other ways than words,
Therefore I scant this breathing courtesy.

GRATIANO
[To NERISSA]
By yonder moon I swear you do me wrong;
In faith, I gave it to the judge's clerk:
Would he were gelt that had it, for my part,
Since you do take it, love, so much at heart.

PORTIA
A quarrel, ho, already! what's the matter?

GRATIANO
About a hoop of gold, a paltry ring
That she did give me, whose posy was

For all the world like cutler's poetry

I will give light, as in joy, but I will not be light, as in promiscuous,
Since a wife who is light in that regard makes her husband heavy-hearted.
Bassanio will never feel that way because of me,
But God will sort it all out. Welcome home, my lord.

Thank you, madam. Please welcome my friend.
This is Antonio, who I told you about—
The one I am forever indebted to.

You should in all senses of the word be indebted to him,
As I hear he was very much indebted to you.

I have been paid back for all of it very well.

Sir, you are very welcome in our house.
But what we see says more than words can,
So I will cut this polite talk short.

[To NERISSA]
By the moon in the sky I swear you've got it wrong. I really did give it to the judge's clerk.
He should have been castrasted, as far as I'm concerned, for as much as it is upsetting you.

An argument already! What is the matter?

It's about a hoop of gold, a trivial ring
That she gave to me that had a little inscription on it
That was nothing more that a knife-maker's

Upon a knife, 'Love me, and leave me not.'

NERISSA
What talk you of the posy or the value?

You swore to me, when I did give it you,
That you would wear it till your hour of death
And that it should lie with you in your grave:

Though not for me, yet for your vehement oaths,
You should have been respective and have kept it.
Gave it a judge's clerk! no, God's my judge,

The clerk will ne'er wear hair on's face that had it.

GRATIANO
He will, an if he live to be a man.

NERISSA
Ay, if a woman live to be a man.

GRATIANO
Now, by this hand, I gave it to a youth,
A kind of boy, a little scrubbed boy,
No higher than thyself; the judge's clerk,
A prating boy, that begg'd it as a fee:
I could not for my heart deny it him.

PORTIA
You were to blame, I must be plain with you,
To part so slightly with your wife's first gift:
A thing stuck on with oaths upon your finger
And so riveted with faith unto your flesh.
I gave my love a ring and made him swear
Never to part with it; and here he stands;
I dare be sworn for him he would not leave it
Nor pluck it from his finger, for the wealth
That the world masters. Now, in faith, Gratiano,
You give your wife too unkind a cause of grief:
An 'twere to me, I should be mad at it.

BASSANIO
[Aside]
Why, I were best to cut my left hand off

---

poem. It said: 'Love me and don't leave me.'

Are you talking about the inscription or the value?
You swore to me, when I gave it to you,
That you would wear it until you died,
And that it would be buried with you in your grave.
If not for me, then for the vows you made,
You should have been respectful and kept it.
You gave it to a judge's clerk! No, as God is my judge—
The 'clerk' you gave it to will never grow hair on their face.

He will if he lives to be a man.

Right, if a woman lives to be a man.

I swear by my hand, I gave it to a young man.
Almost a boy, a little stubby boy—
No taller than you—the judge's clerk,
A boy who talked a lot and begged it as a fee.
I couldn't find it in my heart to say no.

I will speak plainly: you were wrong.
To so easily give away your wife's first gift—
A thing stuck onto your finger with vows,
and fastened with faith to your flesh.
I gave my lover a ring and made him swear
Never to part with it. Here he stands,
And will be so bold to say he would not lose it
Or take it from his finger for all the wealth
In the world. So, to be sure, Gratiano,
You give your wife reason to grieve,
and if it were me, I'd be angry, too.

[Aside]
It would be best if I could cut my left hand off

And swear I lost the ring defending it.

GRATIANO
My Lord Bassanio gave his ring away
Unto the judge that begg'd it and indeed
Deserved it too; and then the boy, his clerk,
That took some pains in writing, he begg'd mine;

And neither man nor master would take aught
But the two rings.

PORTIA
What ring gave you my lord?
Not that, I hope, which you received of me.

BASSANIO
If I could add a lie unto a fault,
I would deny it; but you see my finger
Hath not the ring upon it; it is gone.

PORTIA
Even so void is your false heart of truth.
By heaven, I will ne'er come in your bed
Until I see the ring.

NERISSA
Nor I in yours
Till I again see mine.

BASSANIO
Sweet Portia,
If you did know for whom I gave the ring
And would conceive for what I gave the ring
And how unwillingly I left the ring,

When nought would be accepted but the ring,
You would abate the strength of your displeasure.

PORTIA
If you had known the virtue of the ring,
Or half her worthiness that gave the ring,

Or your own honour to contain the ring,
You would not then have parted with the ring.

And swear I lost the ring defending it.

*Bassanio gave his ring away, as well,
To the judge that asked for it and did, to be
certain, Deserved it. Then the boy, his clerk,
Who took so much trouble in the writings—he
wanted my ring,
And neither man would take anything
But the two rings.*

*Which ring did you give, my lord?
I hope it's not the one I gave to you.*

*If I could lie very well,
I would deny it. But you can see my finger
Does not have a ring on it. It is gone.*

*Your heart is empty of truth.
By heaven, I will never come into your bed
Until I see that ring.*

*I won't come into yours, either,
Until I see my ring again.*

*Sweet Portia,
If you knew who I gave the ring to,
And if you knew who I gave the ring for,
And if you could guess how unwillingly I gave
the ring,
When nothing but the ring would be accepted,
You would not be so unhappy with me.*

*If you had realized the true value of the ring,
Or half the worthiness of the one who gave
you the ring,
Or your honor in keeping the ring—
You would not have parted with the ring.*

Original	Modern
What man is there so much unreasonable, / If you had pleased to have defended it / With any terms of zeal, wanted the modesty / To urge the thing held as a ceremony? / Nerissa teaches me what to believe: / I'll die for't but some woman had the ring.	What man is so unreasonable, / That if you had tried to defend the ring / With any passionate feeling, lacked the restraint / To stop pushing the issue? / Nerissa shows me what to belive: / I'll die before some other woman had the ring.

BASSANIO
No, by my honour, madam, by my soul,
No woman had it, but a civil doctor,

Which did refuse three thousand ducats of me
And begg'd the ring; the which I did deny him
And suffer'd him to go displeased away;
Even he that did uphold the very life

Of my dear friend. What should I say, sweet lady?
I was enforced to send it after him;
I was beset with shame and courtesy;
My honour would not let ingratitude

So much besmear it. Pardon me, good lady;

For, by these blessed candles of the night,
Had you been there, I think you would have begg'd
The ring of me to give the worthy doctor.

PORTIA
Let not that doctor e'er come near my house:
Since he hath got the jewel that I loved,
And that which you did swear to keep for me,
I will become as liberal as you;
I'll not deny him any thing I have,
No, not my body nor my husband's bed:
Know him I shall, I am well sure of it:
Lie not a night from home; watch me like Argus:

If you do not, if I be left alone,
Now, by mine honour, which is yet mine own,
I'll have that doctor for my bedfellow.

NERISSA
And I his clerk; therefore be well advised
How you do leave me to mine own protection.

No, trust me, madam, by my soul—
I didn't give it to a woman but to a doctor of law
I didn't give it to a woman but to a doctor of law who refused to take three thousand ducats from me but begged for the ring, which I denied him and I felt bad about it seeing him go away unhappy.
Of my dear friend. What can I say, sweet lady? I was compelled to send it to him. I was full of shame and in need of good manners. I could not dishonor him by not showing him gratitude—
It would have made me feel bad. Forgive me, good lady.
I swear, by these blessed candles that light the night, If you had been there, I think you would have begged me to give him the ring.

Don't let that legal expert come near my house. Since he has the jewel I loved, And which you did swear to keep for me, I will become as generous as you, And I will not deny him anything. No, not my body or my husband's bed. I wil recognize him—I am sure of it. So, don't spend a night away from home. Watch me like Argus.
If you don't I will be left alone and—by my word, which is still not mine—I will have that legal expert as my lover.

And I will have his clerk. So be advised About leaving me to my own devices.

GRATIANO
Well, do you so; let not me take him, then;
For if I do, I'll mar the young clerk's pen.

Well if you do so, I'd better not catch him, then. If I do, I will damage the young clerk's pen.

ANTONIO
I am the unhappy subject of these quarrels.

I am the reason for these arguments.

PORTIA
Sir, grieve not you;
you are welcome notwithstanding.

*Sir, don't worry—
you are welcome despite all.*

BASSANIO
Portia, forgive me this enforced wrong;
And, in the hearing of these many friends,
I swear to thee, even by thine own fair eyes,
Wherein I see myself—

*Portia, forgive me this error I had to make.
And, within hearing of all of these friends,
I swear to you, by your beautiful eyes
In which I see myself—*

PORTIA
Mark you but that!
In both my eyes he doubly sees himself;
In each eye, one: swear by your double self,

And there's an oath of credit.

*Make sure you hear that!
In both my eyes he twice sees himself.
In each eye, one, and so he's swearing by a double self.
Well, that's a vow you can believe, isn't it?*

BASSANIO
Nay, but hear me:
Pardon this fault, and by my soul I swear
I never more will break an oath with thee.

*No, listen to me—
Forgive me this time and I swear by my soul
That I will never again break a vow to you.*

ANTONIO
I once did lend my body for his wealth;
Which, but for him that had your husband's ring,
Had quite miscarried: I dare be bound again,
My soul upon the forfeit, that your lord
Will never more break faith advisedly.

*I once lent my body for his wealth,
Which —without him who has your husband's ring— I would have lost. I'll risk being promised again, and will give my soul upon forfeit, to guarantee that your lord, will not break a vow with awareness.*

PORTIA
Then you shall be his surety. Give him this
And bid him keep it better than the other.

*Then you will be his guarantor. Give him this
And tell him to keep it better than the other.*

ANTONIO
Here, Lord Bassanio; swear to keep this ring.

Here, Lord Bassanio—swear to keep this ring.

BASSANIO
By heaven, it is the same I gave the doctor!

PORTIA
I had it of him: pardon me, Bassanio;
For, by this ring, the doctor lay with me.

NERISSA
And pardon me, my gentle Gratiano;
For that same scrubbed boy, the doctor's clerk,
In lieu of this last night did lie with me.

GRATIANO *Simile*
Why, this is like the mending of highways
In summer, where the ways are fair enough:
What, are we cuckolds ere we have deserved it?

PORTIA
Speak not so grossly. You are all amazed:
Here is a letter; read it at your leisure;
It comes from Padua, from Bellario:
There you shall find that Portia was the doctor,
Nerissa there her clerk: Lorenzo here
Shall witness I set forth as soon as you
And even but now return'd; I have not yet
Enter'd my house. Antonio, you are welcome;
And I have better news in store for you
Than you expect: unseal this letter soon;
There you shall find three of your argosies
Are richly come to harbour suddenly:
You shall not know by what strange accident
I chanced on this letter.

ANTONIO
I am dumb.

BASSANIO
Were you the doctor and I knew you not?

GRATIANO
Were you the clerk that is to make me cuckold?

NERISSA

Good lord, it is the same one I gave the legal expert!

I got it from him. Forgive me, Bassanio, But I slept with the legal expert for this ring.

And forgive me, my gentle Gratiano— The same stubby boy, the clerk, Gave me this last night to sleep with him.

This is just like fixing roads In the summer when they are good enough. What, we get cheated on before we even deserve it?

Don't speak so blatantly. You are all dumbfounded. Here is a letter: read it slowly. It comes from Padua, from Bellario. In it you will find that Portia was the legal expert, and Nerissa was her clerk. Lorenzo Will testify that I left the house as soon as you And just now returned. I haven't even Entered the house yet. Antonio, you are welcome here, And I have better news for you Than you will expect. Open your letter soon And you will find that three of your ships Have come into harbor, full of riches. I can not say by what strange chance I came upon this letter.

I have no idea what to say.

You were the legal expert and I didn't know it?

You were the clerk that is to cheat on me with my wife?

Ay, but the clerk that never means to do it,
Unless he live until he be a man.

BASSANIO
Sweet doctor, you shall be my bed-fellow:
When I am absent, then lie with my wife.

ANTONIO
Sweet lady, you have given me life and living;

For here I read for certain that my ships
Are safely come to road.

PORTIA
How now, Lorenzo!
My clerk hath some good comforts too for you.

NERISSA
Ay, and I'll give them him without a fee.
There do I give to you and Jessica,
From the rich Jew, a special deed of gift,
After his death, of all he dies possess'd of.

LORENZO
Fair ladies, you drop manna in the way
Of starved people.

PORTIA
It is almost morning,
And yet I am sure you are not satisfied
Of these events at full. Let us go in;
And charge us there upon inter'gatories,
And we will answer all things faithfully.

GRATIANO
Let it be so: the first inter'gatory
That my Nerissa shall be sworn on is,
Whether till the next night she had rather stay,

Or go to bed now, being two hours to day:

But were the day come, I should wish it dark,

Yes, but the clerk will never be able to do it
Unless he grows to be a man.

Sweet expert, you will be my bed-fellow.
When I am away, you can sleep with my wife.

Sweet lady, you have given me life and a reason to live,
For here I read for certain that my ships,
Are coming home saftely.

Well, Lorenzo!
My clerk has some comfort to offer to you, too.

Yes, and I will give them with no interest.
Here, I give to you and Jessica
A special deed of gift from the rich Jew
Which leaves you all he owns after he dies.

Beautiful ladies, you drop bread from heaven to starving people.

It is almost morning,
But I sure you are not yet satisfied
With all of these events. Let's go inside,
And there you can ask us questions
And we will answer all things truthfully.

Let's do that. My first question
For Nerissa to be sworn to answer is
Whether she would rather wait until tomorrow night
Or go to bed now, with only two hours left until morning.
If the day were to come, I would wish it was still dark,

That I were couching with the doctor's clerk.

Well, while I live I'll fear no other thing
So sore as keeping safe Nerissa's ring.

And that I were sleeping with the expert's clerk.
Well, as long as I live I'll fear nothing else
As much as I will fear keeping Nerissa's ring safe.

Exeunt

Made in the USA
Coppell, TX
19 October 2021